"No one will bear to look at you as you meet your gruesome end."

MINNALIS

"There's no way we can stop here. We've only just begun."

KAITO UKEI

The Hero Laughs While Walking the Path of VENGEANCE a Second Time

1 The Traitorous Princess

NERO KIZUKA

Illustration by SINSORA

YEN
ON

NEW YORK

The Hero Laughs While Walking the Path of VENGEANCE a Second Time

1

NERO KIZUKA

TRANSLATION BY JAKE HUMPHREY • COVER ART BY SINSORA

NIDOME NO YUSHA WA FUKUSHU NO MICHI O WARAI AYUMU Vol.1
URAGIRI OJO
©Kizuka Nero 2016
First published in Japan in 2016 by KADOKAWA CORPORATION, Tokyo.
English translation rights arranged with KADOKAWA CORPORATION, Tokyo, through TUTTLE-MORI AGENCY, INC., Tokyo.

Yen On
150 W 30th Street, 19th Floor
New York, NY 10001

Visit us at yenpress.com • facebook.com/yenpress • twitter.com/yenpress
yenpress.tumblr.com • instagram.com/yenpress

First Yen On Edition: December 2021

Yen On is an imprint of Yen Press, LLC.
The Yen On name and logo are trademarks of Yen Press, LLC.

Library of Congress Cataloging-in-Publication Data
Names: Kizuka, Nero, author. | Sinsora, illustrator. | Humphrey, Jake, translator.
Title: The hero laughs while walking the path of vengeance a second time / Nero Kizuka ; illustration by Sinsora ; translation by Jake Humphrey.
Other titles: Nidome no yusha wa fukushuu no michi wo warai ayumu. English
Description: First Yen On edition. | New York, NY : Yen On, 2021.
Identifiers: LCCN 2021038196 | ISBN 9781975323707 (v. 1 ; trade paperback)
Subjects: LCGFT: Fantasy fiction. | Light novels.
Classification: LCC PL872.5.I97 N5313 2021 | DDC 895.63/6—dc23
LC record available at https://lccn.loc.gov/2021038196

ISBNs: 978-1-9753-2370-7 (paperback)
978-1-9753-2371-4 (ebook)

1 3 5 7 9 10 8 6 4 2

LSC-C

Printed in the United States of America

1

The
Traitorous
Princess

The Hero Laughs While Walking the Path of VENGEANCE a Second Time

NERO KIZUKA

CONTENTS

"We'll punish them all. We will show them no mercy."

"Let's think long and hard and come up with the **cruelest** form of **revenge** we can."

PROLOGUE

They were filthy, foul, and nauseating.

The people around me made me sick to my stomach.

They smiled as they stabbed me in the back, grinned as they trod on my kindness, and laughed as they filled my glass with poison. To think I fought so hard for them. What an idiot I'd been. I wish I could go back and punch myself in the face, but it's too late for that now.

It's all over.

I guess you could make the argument that it was my fault for not being smart enough to realize this sooner. Maybe this was inevitable.

But I'm not convinced.

As my lifeblood dripped from the blade sticking out of my chest, I looked around at my former friends—no, at those things I thought were my friends.

"…We did it."

"Geez, what a monster."

"Now it's over. The evil has been vanquished, as God willed."

Why did I ever trust these lying snakes? All I wanted to do was believe in people, and for that, I paid the price. If I get a second chance, I won't make the same mistake. Next time, I'll make sure they all die.

*   *   *

Kill the princess. Kill the knights. Kill the villagers. Kill the wizard. Kill the fighter. Kill the priestess. Kill the martial artist. Kill the assassin. Kill the dancer. Kill the merchant. Kill the king. Kill the queen. Kill the aristocrat.

I would see them all perish. Make them suffer as much as possible. I would take this grudge and etch it deeply onto my heart, so that I would never, ever forget it.

System message: "Holy Sword of Retribution" unlocked.

As my consciousness faded into nothingness, I heard a voice. My body, however, would not move a centimeter.

"Hey, where did we go wrong? ...Why couldn't we stay in those good times forever? Was there nothing we could have done? ...If we meet again, could we do things differently...?"

I remembered the face of the girl I'd been forced to kill. She lay impaled as I was now, a powerless smile on her face. She was the one they'd called evil.

"Heh. Ah-ha— *Hack*— Kah-ha-ha-ha-ha!" I cackled as I coughed up blood. It really was a laughable affair. They had called her the enemy—*my* enemy, but in the end, she'd been my only real friend. Even a clown couldn't have devised a more pathetic outcome.

"Ack! You're still alive?!"

"Fret not. He has no strength remaining. The purification, however, will require a little more time."

"I suppose so. All he can do now is glare at us."

I felt their sneering looks. They were right. The blood loss was already causing my thoughts to blur. What I said next was more of an instinctual reaction than anything else.

"Oh man, I am going to kill you all…"
Then I heard a click, and my HP reached zero. My mind was dragged into oblivion. I died, and Kaito Ukei was no more.

System message: Tutorial mode complete.
Elapsed time: 04 years, 98 days, 17 hours, 52 minutes, 35 seconds.

Regressing level based on time elapsed.
Regression rate exceeds current level. Resetting to initial values…
Remaining 20,000 EXP applied as debt.
Setting level caps at multiples of 10, unlockable via experience.

Regression rate exceeds maximum allowable debt.
Applying excess regression to skills. Revoking/regressing skills…
Skill revocation/regression successful. Skills have been reset to initial values.

Regression rate exceeds available skills.
Applying excess regression to intrinsic ability "Soul Blade."
Revoking soul blades…

…Operation failed because of "Holy Sword of Retribution."

Revocation failed. Switching to experience locking.
Experience lock successful. 53 of 58 soul blades locked.

Excess regression rate satisfied.

Returning to starting location… Complete.
Return to starting location successful.

CHAPTER 1
Laughing at the
World a Second Time

Thank you for coming, Hero. I— *Guph!*"

As soon as I opened my eyes, I instinctively threw a punch at the vile object of hatred standing before me. My fist landed square in the princess's stomach, and Alicia Orollea's silver hair fluttered as she staggered back and kneeled down, clutching herself in pain.

It was a totally opportunistic, half-assed attack. I wanted to punch her right in her pretty little face, but my position on the ground made it impossible to land a good hit.

""Y-Your Highness!""

The royal knights were stunned, unable to process what they'd just seen. They rushed to her side, administering a low-level healing spell that enveloped the princess in a pale light.

I was left feeling dissatisfied. My attack was far weaker than I'd imagined, and I couldn't think of a reason why. Sure, I was unarmed, with no buffs or enchantments (or *luck*, it seemed), but so was she, and she wasn't wearing armor, either.

Once I realized that issue, another thought came to mind.

"Hmm? Wait, what's going on? Is this a dream? Is my life flashing before my eyes?"

I thought I had died, but when I looked down at my body, there was nothing wrong with me. The Immortal-Slaying Blade, the sword that killed me, was nowhere to be found. Even more concerning, my clothes were completely different.

I was still wearing the black school uniform I used four years ago, when I, Kaito Ukei, first came to this land.

"What are you doing, you cur?!"

"Hero or not, nobody harms Her Royal Highness!"

The royal knights brandished their weapons, but I could tell they wouldn't attack. The old me, unused to combat, could never have read their intentions so easily, but now they were like open books.

So I ignored them, continuing to take in my surroundings. I was in the summoning chamber within the royal castle. Just a moment ago, I had been in the Dragon Crypt, the inner sanctum of the Dragon Temple.

But the Dragon Temple lay at the farthest reaches of the world. The two locations must have been about ten thousand kilometers apart. It would take at least a dozen reactivations to teleport over that sort of distance, and even the demon lord, who boasted unrivaled magical prowess, couldn't make the trip in one go.

…Which meant this must be my life flashing before my eyes. But then why did it feel so real? Why could I think so calmly and rationally? And the feel of that punch, and the guard's eyes… It was all too clear to be a dream. If it was neither a dream nor my life flashing before my eyes, then unfortunately, I was out of ideas. Nothing could explain the situation I was in now.

"Hey, are you even listening to me?!" asked a knight.

"Nope," I replied.

"What?! You insolent dog!"

My candid reply must have injured his pride, for he instantly stopped yammering. Now the way he held his sword told me he meant to use it. Though my mind was still hazy, my body leaped into action immediately, responding to the threat.

"Huh? Guplgh!"

I stepped forward and planted my weight on my front foot, launching my elbow into the guard's throat with everything in me. For three years, I had trained and fought to defeat the demon lord. After that, the world decided it no longer needed me, and I spent a year being made a scapegoat for their problems. To survive that long, I learned to react with lethal force to any perceived threat.

The other guards stopped in their tracks at this unprecedented turn of events. The one I struck fell back against the wall, his throat crushed, mouth foaming. He appeared to be having a little accident down below, too.

"Oh? I'm surprised that didn't decapitate you. Is that a spirit-reinforced neck plate? Hmm, no, I don't sense any magic. You know, my body feels heavy. Hmm?"

In the deathly silent room, I was the only one speaking.

My opponent was a run-of-the-mill knight, not exactly some expert warrior. Even my unarmed attacks should have dealt more damage than this. That should have bent his head backward ninety degrees or more.

"Ro-Roland!"

After a few seconds, one of the other knights overcame his shock and rushed to his side, quickly reciting a healing spell. When he realized that wouldn't be enough, he reached for his belt and administered a more advanced healing potion.

"Wh-whatever is the matter, Hero? D-did we displease you...?" stammered the princess, her face pale. When I heard her voice, my rage became palpable, and everyone in the room froze in response to it.

"You bet your ass I'm displeased, Alicia. I hate everything about you: your voice, your eyes, your heart and soul. I hate you inside and out. You make me sick. I want to vomit after hearing the word *hero* spoken by the likes of you."

The sense of impending danger whipped the royal knights into action, and they moved to protect their princess. However, there was no point in them doing so. After all, none of them were fast enough to stop me.

"Eek! Ack! Ghgh!"

My body felt strangely slow as I slipped between the guards to grab the princess by the throat and slam her against the wall.

"You summoned an innocent human to be your hero. You made me do whatever you asked. Then once the sorceress was gone, you turned your sights on me and stabbed me in the back without ever breaking your perfect smile."

"Wh-what are you talking abou—? Ghk!"

What a joke. Did she think I'd forgotten? The moment we triumphed over evil, the world double-crossed me. The priestess painted me as the enemy, and the kingdom followed suit, pinning all their crimes on me. I'd fought alongside them. I thought they were my friends, but they betrayed me—all of them. My reward for trusting them blindly, for believing their story and agreeing to save them, was for them to throw stones, abuse me, and spit on me.

This princess was one of them. After the sorceress fell, the world changed. I didn't know who was on my side anymore. That was when she came to me. She told me she'd protect me, and tired as I was from a life on the run, I believed her. Then she double-crossed me, laughing all the while. She gave me a teleportation stone and promised that it would take me to safety, but it was a trap, leading to a room in a dungeon from which I could not return. I barely escaped with my life, and the wounds I sustained in the process took a long time to heal.

"Oh, I still remember what you said to me back then. 'It's not a betrayal. I was never on your side to begin with.' As though other-worlders don't even register as human beings to you."

"I really...don't know what you're talking about..."

She was making a fool of me. And what a fool I had been. If I hadn't been so blinded by "trust" and just looked at her and taken the time to be skeptical, I would have noticed her true intentions before it was too late. Even now, as her face paled with terror and pain, I could sense the evil lurking deep inside. I could see it in her body language, her gaze, her breathing, and the minute changes in her facial expressions. On the battlefield, such things betrayed your next move. Here, they betrayed the princess's true thoughts to me.

"Heh. You're good at playing dumb; I'll give you that. I don't know what's going on here, or if this is a dream or what, but I don't care. I'll think about that later." A sigh escaped my lips. "I don't know how much extra time I have, and I did swear an oath, after all."

My voice overflowed with joy. My face contorted with delight, and my heart beat faster and faster, my arms growing restless.

"Ah... Ugh..."

Then any hostility I detected from the princess disappeared. I released my grip, allowing her to fall to the ground, and she looked back up at me with fear in her eyes. I saw myself reflected in her pupils, a twisted expression plastered on my face.

But that was okay, because I finally got to live in a simple world where I could be the hero, only for that world to betray me and call me the enemy. It was the punch line to a sick joke. Who wouldn't laugh at that? The pure-minded fool I had been was long dead, and I lived only for revenge. Now with my sworn enemy lying right at my feet, how else was I supposed to look?

"Please...please help me..."

"No. I want to see you suffer, Alicia."

"Gah!"

I pummeled her face. Right. Left. Right. Left. Prolonging her agony as much as possible without knocking her out.

"You scoundrel!"

"Gurh!"

"Come, now. Is that all you've got? Your precious princess is getting beaten up, and that's all you can do?"

The knights overcame their fear and leaped to her defense, but a mere half dozen guards were no match for me. I struck their joints, throwing them off balance and sending them crashing to the ground as painfully as I could.

I threw my weight on top of them, twisting and breaking bones. I gouged out their eyes, tore their ears, and ripped their noses.

"Ah-ha-ha! Ah-ha-ha-ha-ha!"

My body still felt heavy, but I didn't draw my soul blade just yet. A sword would end things too quickly, and I wasn't only trying to kill them; I wanted vengeance. I wanted them to suffer a long and painful death. Only then would I feel at ease.

"Ah-ha-ha-ha-ha-ha-ha-ha-ha!"

Their terrified screams of agony were like music to my ears. The sound excited me. I made sure not to inflict any fatal wounds, and they continued to scream as the pain kept them awake.

For the guards and the princess, this must have been hell.

But for me, it was a paradise where all my wishes were granted.

I couldn't stop my laughter, and they couldn't stop their screams.

"Ahhh... Urgh... Gah..."

"Hgh... Gh... Ah..."

When at last only the sound of weak groans filled the room and any further torture failed to elicit a response, I stopped. Princess Alicia lay on the floor before me, her face so bloodied and bruised that she was nearly unrecognizable. Each one of her fingers had been bent backward and broken, and her stare was vacant, her mouth frothing at the edges.

"Now, let's find out what's going on here," I said.

My thirst for revenge was far from sated, but there was little sense in torturing a victim who could no longer react. My rampage had cleared my mind a bit, and once I could think clearly, I summoned one of my soul blades. Resisting the urge to impale Alicia with it right then and there, I cast a healing spell on her instead. A small amount of mana flowed from my hand and into the pale-white light of the Nephrite Blade of Verdure, a soul-blade form I unlocked in the elven forest.

This dagger had a fifteen-centimeter blade made of some sort of crystal with a greenish hue, and I could channel mana into it to produce a healing effect. However, as it would take a while to bring the princess back to full health, I used the time to confront my suspicions.

"It's not just my imagination; my body really is heavier. Why?" I wondered. It was clear from the fight that my physical ability had dropped. "Oh, perhaps that curse's effect is still active?"

The Immortal-Slaying Blade, the sword that ran me through. Every hit applied a debuff that lowered the target's base ability scores. It was the Church's prized relic, and at the time, I had a soul blade equipped that negated its effects.

My intrinsic ability, "Soul Blade," was a weapon that I could command to take on a variety of forms depending on the conditions I had fulfilled. Those four years of training weren't just for show. Among all the blades I had collected, I knew there was one that nullified status conditions. To find out which one it was, I needed only to look.

"Open Status."

At the sound of my voice, a semitransparent blue screen appeared. My status screen. These showed the abilities of whoever invoked them, but they were incorporeal, and barring certain kinds of skills or magic, only the person to whom the screen belonged could see the information written there.

What I read was shocking.

"…What the hell?"

I thought it was a bug. I rubbed my eyes, closed the screen, shook my head, and tried again.

"Open Status."

Kaito Ukei　　Lv1

Age 17 • Male

HP: 531/545　　MP: 347/412

Strength: 224　　Stamina: 324

Vitality: 545　　Dexterity: 587

Magic: 117　　Resistance: 497

Intrinsic Abilities: Soul Blade ▽, Auto-Translate

Skills: Unarmed Lv 1

Status: OK

"...Why?"

There was so much wrong with what I saw, but that one question was all I could muster.

Firstly, my age. I arrived in this world four years ago, when I was still a second-year in high school. Back then, I was seventeen. I was supposed to be twenty-one now. Was this some sort of age-reversing magic? Impossible.

But that wasn't the real problem. Next was my level. After defeating the demon lord, I had continued to gain experience, passed level 300, and was approaching 400. Just to put that in perspective, the most powerful knight in the kingdom, the commander of the royal knight order, was level 121 when he joined my quest. By the time it was over, he was level 270.

Obviously, the higher your level, the higher your stats. I knew of levels dropping because of age or missed training, but I'd never heard of losing over 300 levels at once. In this world, level 1 was like a baby. I was already level 3 when I first arrived. Now I was level 1, and my stats had taken a big hit.

And finally, my skills. Intrinsic abilities were either innate or were awarded for fulfilling special conditions, such as becoming a hero. Skills, on the other hand, could be learned by anyone if they followed the correct procedure. This meant that in theory, you could learn any skill given enough time, though in practice, people tended to specialize. Skills had proficiency and levels, and the only way to improve a skill was by using it repeatedly, building up proficiency until your level increased.

All the skills I'd devoted the last four years of my life to mastering had been replaced with a single word: *Unarmed.*

"Wh-what the hell? *Air Step!*"

Although most of her wounds had healed, the princess still hadn't regained consciousness. Regardless, I interrupted the healing spell and put away my soul blade. Leaping up, I created a floating platform of magic and kicked off it. The skill I randomly picked to test, "Air Step," involved creating magical stepping stones in the air to facilitate aerial combat. It was indispensable in battle, and fortunately, it had activated. However...

"You have got to be joking..."

...the pitiful result left me lost for words. The MP consumption and cooldown rate were nowhere near what I was used to.

"Open Status!"

The status screen had been appended with the skills I had just used, Air Step and "Control Mana." I tapped the words *Air Step* and sighed.

"I knew it..."

STATUS

Kaito Ukei   Lv1

Age 17 • Male

HP: 531/545   MP: 297/412

Strength: 224   Stamina: 324

Vitality: 545   Dexterity: 587

Magic: 117   Resistance: 497

Intrinsic Abilities: Soul Blade ▽, Auto-Translate
Skills: Unarmed Lv 1, Control Mana Lv 1,
Air Step Lv 1
Status: OK

Air Step—Skill Level: 1

Skill Proficiency: 1/10,000

Creates floating platforms of magic.

The status screen floated gently in the air as I tried to digest its contents. It was behaving as though I had only just acquired the skill now. The huge chunk of MP I lost from trying to use the skill was even more proof. As I explained previously, your skill level indicates how much you have gotten used to using that skill. By using a skill successfully, you increase your proficiency and, eventually, your level, allowing you to execute the skill more efficiently. Practice makes perfect, in other words.

With Air Step, increasing the level reduced MP consumption and decreased the time required between activations. A skill at level 1 was, to put it bluntly, absolute trash. The MP consumption was so high that it wasn't even worth using it in battle. I tried a few other skills, just to make sure, but they were all at level 1, too.

"There's no way this is all from the curse. If the effect had been this great, that battle would have been over immediately."

The only reason I had ever survived a year on my own was because Air Step, Control Mana—hell, pretty much everything—were at such a high level that using them was as natural to me as breathing. Assuming, that is, that everything up to the point when I woke up in this room even happened.

If that sword could undo skill progression like this, the kingdom wouldn't have needed a hero to beat the demon lord. They could have killed her easily enough without me—if not immediately, then certainly without great effort.

"Perhaps after I died... Well, I suppose I'm alive, so maybe they put some new status condition on me to save me?"

The status screen had said I was *OK*, but there were so many other problems with the information it showed that I hesitated to consider it a reliable source. Besides, it might even be some kind of advanced hex that could change the screen itself. However, there was a soul blade I could use that would ascertain exactly what kind of status condition this was. It allowed for an even greater level of detail than the status screen. If this really was some hitherto unknown condition, this soul blade would tell me its effects, and how to counteract it.

"Now then, Appraise... App...raise?"

As I went to search my status screen for the soul blade in question, I paused.

"There's no way..."

I cringed as I considered a worrisome thought and pressed the down arrow beside the soul-blade display. The names of all the forms that had taken me through so many hardships were there. However, most of them were grayed out, with a small padlock icon beside them. When I tapped the lock, the form's name and the requirements to unlock the weapons appeared.

"This can't be happening..."

I tried to summon some of the soul blades that were grayed out, but none of them worked. Only the ones whose names were displayed in bright-white text were available to me.

I rubbed my eyes once more and stared. As my anger and frustration threatened to boil over, I turned to the princess on the ground, who for a while now had been pretending to be unconscious while muttering a spell under her breath. I gave her a swift kick.

"Gaaaagh?!"

"You really are sneaky, Alicia. Why do you think I've been healing you? Don't go dying before I can finish torturing you, now."

The spell she had been chanting was a low-level Fire spell. When I interrupted her, it went off inside the princess's mouth. It must have hurt. I smiled. I didn't say it, but I enjoyed watching her resist, as long as she wasn't trying to off herself too early. I loved beating down her attempts and seeing her drive herself deeper into despair. It was very entertaining.

Just as I was thinking what a relief it was to finally see the princess suffer for what she'd done, I noticed a mysterious mail icon sitting in the upper left of my status screen. I had never seen it before and was unsure what it meant.

"Hmm, what to do...?"

"Gh... Gablgh..."

I idly trampled Princess Alicia's stomach with my foot, enjoying how unseemly she looked and sounded as she glared at me in anger. After a short while, when I recovered from the shock of losing almost all my soul blades, I tapped the mail icon with my finger.

If you are reading this, it means you have died an untimely death.

I'm afraid this isn't a joke. You are, without a doubt, well and truly dead. Or rather, you would be, had I not rewound time back to the point of your arrival once your HP reached zero.

You see, what you have been experiencing up until now is called "Tutorial Mode."

When a human arrives in another world, the field they pass through imparts unto them what we on Earth might call superpowers. These powers tend to be stronger than those possessed by the natives of the other world. Yet even so, humans from Earth live, on average, much shorter lives than natives. They die almost immediately, in fact, regardless of what powers they get.

As Goddess of Earth, I do not know the world you have ended up in, and I have no power there. As such, in times past, I would warn humans to be careful. However, the ways of other worlds can be difficult for humans to grasp, and few are able to adapt.

Thus, I stopped trying to warn them. Instead, I created Tutorial Mode.

I understand that it must be difficult to be thrust into this situation with no explanation, but seeing is believing, as they say. Tutorial Mode is my final gift to you, as Goddess of Earth.

In the event of a premature death, time is rewound to the precise moment of arrival. Any skills and levels earned are deducted at a rate based on the time spent alive.

You might call it a "New Game Plus" of sorts. You may not be physically stronger the second time around, but your trials have taught you an important lesson about how easy it is to die. That is my gift to you.

The humans of Earth possess very little magic ability, and an individual human is exceedingly weak. Frankly, they are the bottom-feeders of the universe. Human stats are barely above baseline, but the power they obtain when crossing worlds makes them just about strong enough to defeat a slime. Without that power, even an expert martial artist from Earth would lose to an otherworld's lowliest villager.

Therefore, you must steel yourself to survive. The worlds beyond Earth are rife with danger around every corner. I sincerely apologize that I can do no more for you.

From the Goddess

*　　*　　*

"I see. *New Game Plus*, huh?"

Just as the shape of the icon suggested, what I had just read appeared to be a letter. There was a lot written there that I wanted to unpack, but first: There was a Goddess. And levels and skills seemed to also exist in my previous world, Earth.

From what I could gather, even ridiculously strong abilities couldn't prevent earthlings from getting themselves killed, so the Goddess resorted to a strategy best summed up as *Let them figure it out for themselves, and they can have one do-over for free.*

That was what saved me. I still had my doubts, but that was what the letter said. And that explained why my skill levels had tanked; it was because I had lived so long.

...In any case.

"Ha-ha..."

Thank the heavens. Now I could carry out the oath I swore.

"MUA-HA-HA-HA-HA!"

All I could do was laugh. I couldn't help myself. Even though I never actually expected to be given another chance, the oath I swore was not a lie. A shiver of delight ran through my body. This wasn't a dream. I had as long as I liked to exact my revenge.

When I finally finished laughing, I considered the matter more calmly. What to do, and where to begin? There were so many people I wanted to kill. One of them lay right there at my feet.

Right now, her mouth was burned, and I had stamped on her so much that her dress was ragged and dirty. She understood now that it made no difference whether or not she obeyed. She simply looked up at me with hate in her eyes.

Yes. That was it. I wanted revenge. If I just wanted to give in to my urges, I could kill her whenever. After all, their levels had been reset, too, just like mine. However, I still had the knowledge that I learned from the tutorial. I might have lost my skill levels, but I didn't lose my memory.

Thanks to my few usable soul blades, I had about fifty levels worth of stat boosts, and I could easily handle myself against a half dozen enemies who had never seen real combat, as the knights groaning around me showed. All I had to do was lay low for a little while, raise my level, and then go around picking off those bastards before they had the chance to get stronger.

"Oh, wait, no. That won't do."

For a year, I had suffered. I had been torn apart—splintered—and the pieces rearranged to form the creature I was now. My soul had been stained black with tar, and it screamed at me not to just kill them. It wouldn't let me. So as much as I hated the look of her, I wasn't anywhere near finished with the princess yet.

She could live for now. There was still much to do.

There was no need to rush. I had all the time in the world. Why kill her now and let it end? Make her suffer. Drag her down into a swamp of despair and let her rue the day she ever crossed me. There was so much more I wanted her to experience. My revenge hadn't even begun.

"Oh dear, I suppose I can't kill you yet. What a shame; I'd come up with such good ideas for how to do it, too."

I sighed. It really was a shame. I wanted to watch maggots devour her from the inside out. I wanted to implant her with a seed that slowly converted her flesh to plant matter, until she was nothing but a mind trapped inside a numb, unmoving body. However, even if I did want to kill her right now, I had lost access to the soul blades I required. I needed more time. Time to plan out my revenge—thoroughly, so that I could enjoy the process.

"First…" I used the Nephrite Blade of Verdure to heal the princess's mouth so that she could talk. "Hey, I have a favor to ask you," I said.

"…Why should I listen to a monster?" spat the princess. What a perfect specimen she was.

"Ha-ha-ha-ha!"

"Wh-what's so funny?" she asked.

"Oh, that was just such a good response. Please don't lose that defiance, Princess. I wouldn't want things to get boring."

I sneered down at her pitiable form as she shot back a wicked glare.

"You madman! Why are you doing this? What did I ever do to you…?!"

"You may not remember, Princess, but I do. I know the pain that comes with betrayal. You tricked me. You betrayed me. You played me for a fool. I believed in you guys. Do you have any idea how much that hurt, Alicia Orollea?"

"Ugh… Ghuh…"

My eyes seared right through her skin like magma, and my tongue was razor-sharp. She may not have known what I was talking about, but she understood that I hated her guts all the same.

"Now, back to the point. The favor."

I shot her a perfect smile without the slightest trace of the animosity I had been showing her before.

"It's okay if you don't want to do it. I tried asking nicely, even patched up your mouth for you, but if you still don't want to, then it's okay."

Oh, you think I knew that she would refuse all along? I don't know what you're talking about! I never imagined for a moment she might reject my earnest request.

"Wh-what?"

Upon seeing my personality totally switch, the princess became worried. She always had been a sharp one.

"Hmm, your tits are in the way."

"Huh?! Eek! Sto...stop that!"

I kicked her over onto her front and tore at her dress, exposing the bare skin of her back.

"You know, the first time I met you, I thought you were so beautiful, but now I don't feel anything. Isn't that strange?"

Silver hair that cascaded down to her shoulders, and a pair of glimmering silver eyes. Her face, her body—they were all perfect, like a doll. She was truly a girl worthy of being called "the Beauty of Orollea." When I first arrived, I had thought her prettier than any girl I had ever seen in my native country of Japan, and the few times I saw her undress on our journey made my heart pound.

Yet now as I looked upon her delicate physique, I felt nothing.

"You would defile a helpless maiden? I knew otherworlders were a load of brutish savages!"

"Huh? What *are* you talking about? Who would want to screw a pig with an ugly personality? Don't flatter yourself."

The thought of actually doing it made my stomach turn, and I responded with pure vitriol.

"Wha...?!"

"I'm simply going to write a letter, since you didn't want to do me a favor."

"...You...you don't mean..."

"Look, all I wanted was for you to take a message. It wasn't difficult, was it? If you don't want to, then I'm just going to have to write it down where everyone can see."

As I watched her slowly realize what I was going to do to her, I cracked a smile.

"Now, hold still, Princess. Wouldn't want to mess up my handwriting."

"No! Aaaahhhh!"

I took out the Pyrachnid's Claw of Kindling. A twenty-five-centimeter short sword with a relatively wide, crimson blade. If we consider this the second time I was using this weapon, then the first time I wielded it was only to light tinder. Its heat was weak, but right now, that was exactly what I needed.

"Hmm, hmm, hmm, hmmm! ♪"

"Gyah! Graaagh! Aaaauuuugh! Stop! Stopppp!"

I seared my message into Alicia's back, humming over the sound of her screams.

"Zo...zomeone...blease helb..."

"Ah-ha-ha! Nobody's coming to save you, Princess. I've made sure you have no more tricks up your sleeve."

Alicia reached her arms out toward the knights who lay around her, but none of them responded. Their arms and legs were broken and mangled, bent backward at the joints. Though they were conscious, the sheer pain they were in deafened them to the princess's cries.

"Now hold still. I'm not even half done yet, and there's a lot more I've got in store for you after this," I said, smiling.

By the time I finished writing my letter, I was in a good mood, and everyone else in the room had fallen silent. I had broken the princess's limbs to stop her from struggling, and in the end, she had passed out a little while ago from the pain. Even the knights lay still as one by one, they, too, had given themselves up to merciful stupor. I began to stand up, and my vision blurred.

"Whoa. It's been a while since I've felt this way."

It was a sign that my MP was wearing thin. I had been using the Pyrachnid's Claw of Kindling in conjunction with the Nephrite Blade of Verdure to keep Princess Alicia alive. The former didn't use much MP, but the healing ability of the latter burned through it.

"Open Status."

I checked, and my MP had dropped to about 20 percent. It looked like I would have to be frugal in my use of the soul blades. I wouldn't be able to fight like I used to until I regained my MP-recovery and cost-reduction skills. I needed to make it a priority to level up as soon as possible.

"Well, whatever. I suppose I should get going."

I had done everything I wanted to here. It was time to slip out of the castle, get some things together, and put this city behind me.

"...You can't. You'll never leave this castle alive."

"Oh, you're still awake?"

"Over five hundred knights are stationed within its grounds. You'll be tortured and killed."

The repeated wounding and healing must have rendered her body numb, because Princess Alicia's voice sounded clear, unaffected by pain. A defiant fire had returned to her cold, mocking eyes. Trust a princess to still hold up after rounds of torture. Though I knew she didn't fully understand the situation and was mostly putting on a brave face, she would be right as rain with a little time, and I could have all the fun I wanted then. I was getting giddy. My contemplative silence gave Alicia the mistaken impression that her words had actually worried me, and she continued:

"We show you foul outsiders a hint of kindness, and you try to take advantage of it. Oh, you will pay for this humiliation. I will pay you back one hundredfold and have you beg for death!"

Her eyes shone with pure unbridled rage. Yes, this was what I wanted to see. Those eyes. The look you only got when you realized

Kaito Ukei

Lv1

Age 17 • Male

HP: 531/545   MP: 81/412

Strength: 224   Stamina: 324

Vitality: 545   Dexterity: 587

Magic: 117   Resistance: 497

Intrinsic Abilities: Soul Blade ▽, Auto-Translate
Skills: Unarmed Lv 1, Control Mana Lv 1,
Air Step Lv 1
Status: OK

you'd been screwed over. That was enough to show me just how much pain and humiliation I'd inflicted on her.

The princess went on. "Perhaps if you cry and beg at my feet, I'll spare you such a miserable death. After all, I could still use a hero like you. If you swear allegiance to me, I'll let you live a life of luxury as a hero among my people. Wouldn't that be an honor?"

I snorted. As soon as she had the chance, she began lording over me. It was blatantly obvious from her words and mannerisms that she thought she still had the upper hand.

"Haaaaahhhh…"

A deep, long, drawn-out sigh emerged from the bottom of my lungs. What an idiot I must have been to ever think I was friends with a girl like her. I could cry if I wanted to. There was no way in hell I was going to beg for mercy like she asked, but even if I did, I knew the princess would never keep her word. I could see she was just slavering at the idea of putting me in my place, using me as her pawn, and then torturing me to death once she was done with me.

I always thought she was a brainless beauty who could be tricked into doing anything, but I guess I was even more brainless, seeing how I had been completely wrapped around her little finger.

There was one other thing: It was clear that the pain she felt was nowhere near the level where it would satisfy my thirst for vengeance. She was still thinking about how she might manipulate me to her benefit. I wanted her to be so depraved, driven so utterly mad by my actions, that all she could think about was getting her hands on me and killing me. It was going to take a lot of time and effort to reach that stage, and there was still an incredible number of people I wanted to get revenge on.

But that suits me just fine. It means I can take my time and enjoy it!

The corners of my mouth twisted into a smile as I thought of what was to come.

"Wh-why are you smiling? I'm not lying about the knights!"

"Oh, I believe you. But they haven't responded to all the noise we've been making in here, have they? That's because the walls are soundproofed, warded, fortified—you name it. Anything to safeguard the secrets of the summoning ritual. What's more, you ordered that nobody disturb this place until the ritual was complete."

"H-how did you…?!"

"Because *you told me last time.*"

The princess stared at me, wide-eyed in astonishment.

"Well then, I'm off," I said curtly.

I strode over to the edge of the room, where I grabbed a mounted sconce and pulled it toward me. A large block of stone in the wall of the summoning chamber rattled open, and a passage appeared that led up a flight of stairs.

"Only those of royal blood know about that secret stairway! How did you—?"

"I told you: I've been here before."

She was the one, after all, who had led me back here, offering me refuge. She told me about the hidden passage right before she betrayed me.

"Oh, whoopsie-daisy. I almost forgot."

So enchanted I was by this prelude to the journey of my revenge that something had slipped my mind. I walked over to one of the knights, who by now more closely resembled a macabre art piece than a human being.

"I was going to do this with my bare hands, but you taught me such a splendid way of silencing people that I just have to try it out. My MP is looking a little low, but it should be more than enough for this."

I took out the Pyrachnid's Claw of Kindling and produced

a small ball of flame at the tip before dropping it into the knight's mouth and detonating it.

"¢£%#&□△◆■?!"

It wasn't enough to kill him, but the knight produced an inhuman scream as the explosion charred the inside of his mouth black.

"Looking good. Okay, next."

One by one, I performed the same treatment on the other knights. By the time I had finished, they lay there silently, unable to even cry out in pain.

"Now it's your turn, Alicia. I don't suppose we shall see each other for some time. If you have something you want to say to me, now's your last chance."

"...Tell me your name."

"Hey now, I can't do that. How will I lie low if the entire kingdom knows who I am? That's why I signed that *letter* the way I did."

I tossed the ball of flame into the princess's open mouth.

"Call me...The Revenant."

Princess Alicia neither flailed nor screamed as the fire scorched her gullet. She was desperate not to show a shred of weakness. Her fingers were all useless, and her throat would take a while to heal. I had bought myself some time.

"Ah, and I'll take this, too, if you don't mind. Could do with a bit of spending money."

I slipped off the necklace that lay around her neck. She had once told me it was a priceless treasure of the royal family, so it would take care of my financial needs for a while.

Princess Alicia glared at me with hate in her watery eyes. Seeing that made it all seem worthwhile, I thought. I left her with a smile as that pleasing gaze followed me through the secret door and up the stairs.

*   *   *

As I continued through the dark underground passage, I couldn't stop thinking about what I had just said. An old, distant memory came back to haunt me. I sighed in a long, drawn-out way, and then the words began to flow.

"Argh, why couldn't I come up with a better name? Grrrrr! I should have just thought about it some more! I mean, come on. 'The Revenant'? Anything would have been better than that!"

The memories of my cringey teen phase came flooding back and lingered with me like malevolent spirits as I made my way through the darkness.

CHAPTER 2
The Hero Strides Through
the World a Second Time

I pushed the stone aside and exited into the bright outdoors.
"I'M FREEEEEE!"

After the long walk underground, I spread my arms and bathed in the sun's radiant rays. I was in a deserted copse just outside the city. I took several deep breaths, savoring the smell of the sunlit trees and the warm earth. It made a welcome change from the damp subterranean cobblestones of the passage I had just walked.

It had been three months since I last saw the sun, including the time I spent in the Dragon Temple before I died. A tear came to my eye as I beheld its majesty.

"Ahhh, glorious sunlight..."

For a while, I basked in its magnificence beneath the clear blue sky. Then I collected my thoughts. My goal was simple. I would seek out those traitors who double-crossed me and exact my revenge, making each and every one of them suffer for their crimes.

The problem was that I wasn't strong enough to do so yet. I needed more time. Everything had to be in place. At level 1, my stamina was nowhere near enough to take on a castle full of knights, at least not without improving my skills first.

For now, the only people who knew what I looked like were the princess and her knights. Unlike last time, when I was a renowned hero by the time I was on the run, there probably wouldn't be any issue if I simply hid out in the next town over. If not, I could always wear a long robe that covered my face. At least that way, I could enter taverns and shops and maybe even walk down the street without being recognized.

I looked up at the sun once more, which was just slightly dipping in the sky. It triggered a memory of the first time I was summoned; I estimated it to be an hour or so past noon.

"The castle's wizards are skilled, but I bet it'll take at least the rest of the day before the princess can speak or write," I said to myself. "I should have plenty of time, so long as I don't get sidetracked."

I strolled into the city and was greeted with the familiar view of the main street. The citizens here blithely listened to the words of the crown and the Church and believed me to be the enemy. Or at least they did last time around anyway. I couldn't help thinking about how nice it would be if they tripped and cracked their skulls open on the stones, but unlike with the princess, I wasn't driven to immediate violence. Perhaps it was because they weren't responsible for the plot against me—they were just ordinary people who believed what they were told. I had to get my priorities right; there were bigger fish to fry.

After that consideration of my own feelings, I thought about how best to raise some money. I did have one idea. I felt around in the pocket of my old school uniform for the heavy necklace that I pinched off the princess. Even if you discounted the fact that it was a royal treasure, the item itself would fetch a decent price, since it held mithril, colorful magic stones, and an enchantment that imparted a tiny Dexterity boost. If I sold it, I would have enough money to last me a good long while. However, I would need to be cautious. I certainly didn't look the part of a noble, and finding a buyer in the first place would be difficult.

None of the shops around here would do, so I headed elsewhere—to the slums, a quarter of the city that was home to all sorts of misfits and outcasts. As I walked in that direction, the streets gradually became dirtier and more run-down, until I arrived in such a forsaken place that, if I didn't know any better, I would have doubted was still the same town.

Cracks and holes were visible in the walls of the crumbling buildings. The place stank of filth and human waste. The people squatting in the shadows had dark and sullen eyes, and I could feel their glares on me like hyenas awaiting their next meal. Half of them eyed me with fear, the others with curious hunger. The ones who dismissed me out of hand were new. Here, you learned in no time at all that you didn't take people at face value.

"Hey, you there, in the funny clothes. What're you doin' all alone in a place like this?"

"…"

"Well, now. Hate to be the bearer of bad news, but ain't no passage through these parts for free. You want through, you gotta pay the toll. You know the drill."

About half a dozen men closed in on me, grinning.

"God, these clichés… Well, at least I know where things are going."

Why did this always happen when I went to the slums? Sure, my clothes made me stick out like a sore thumb, but it was like they were all reading from the exact same script. I knew from my days on the run how useful the slums were, but if I had to go through this farce every time, I'd lose my damn mind. But what could I do? To them, this really was my first visit here. I just wished they'd shake things up a bit, because this part of the plot got real old, real fast.

The slum residents had already fled the area, not wanting to get dragged into a fight. Smart move. That's how you survive here. Stick around, and you'd better have sharp wits and an equally sharp blade.

"Might as well ask," I muttered before calling out, "Are you my enemies?"

"Huh? The hell are you talking about?"

"Just answer the question. I've got no grievance with you. I'll let you get out of this alive if you leave right now."

"What? Man, I thought you were an idiot walking into this place by yourself, but you're real messed up. Ain't ya got the smarts to figure out what kinda situation you in? Man, we got a real sucker here, boys."

The tanned, bald man who appeared to be the leader of the bunch laughed heartily, and his subordinates followed suit.

"Listen, buddy. Just hand over all your gold. Then we won't kill ya. We'll just sell you as a slave instead!"

"I see, so that's the way it's going to be," I said.

The delinquents all came at me at once, so I stepped forward with the Pyrachnid's Claw of Kindling and, using a swing, severed their legs at the ankles.

"Huh? Hraaaaaarghhh!"

The sudden loss of both their feet sent them into shock, and they collapsed headfirst into the dirt of the unpaved road.

"Who is this freak?! Aaargh! My legs! It hurts! It huuuurts!"

"Grrraaargh! What the...? Gaaaaargh!"

I chose the Pyrachnid's Claw so that I wouldn't get covered in blood. Its searing edge burned and melted flesh, cauterizing wounds immediately.

Last time, my uniform had been damaged early on as the result of a bandit attack. Not long after I threw it away, I came across a soul blade with the power to repair cloth. The irony was not lost on me, and it was painful to remember, even now.

"Hmm. I wonder if that worked. Open Status."

I stood up straight and checked my status screen, ignoring the delinquents' feeble cries as they writhed on the ground behind me. As I expected, I had just gained the skill "Fleet-Foot." Also present was the "Darkvision" skill, which I had picked up in the underground tunnel.

Darkvision, as the name implied, was a skill that allowed you to see better in dark places. Fleet-Foot let you channel mana into your legs to give a temporary boost to your Dexterity stat.

I had attempted to use Fleet-Foot once before, back in the summoning chamber, when I dashed past the guards to grab Alicia by the throat. Back then, I could tell that it had failed to go off because I felt a little recoil damage in my legs. That was why I hadn't gained the skill then and why my HP was a little below full. I still hadn't had time to rest, so my HP wasn't fully restored. My MP, however, which recovered over time, had gone back up to about half. Minus the 30 percent or so it took to execute Fleet-Foot just now, it was currently sitting at around 20 percent. It was going to be hard to train the skill if it required that much MP to use.

"Although…"

Kaito Ukei   Lv 1

Age 17 • Male

HP: 531/545   MP: 75/412

Strength: 224   Stamina: 324

Vitality: 545   Dexterity: 587

Magic: 117   Resistance: 497

**Intrinsic Abilities: Soul Blade ▽, Auto-Translate
Skills: Unarmed Lv 1, Control Mana Lv 1,
Air Step Lv 1, Darkvision Lv 2, Fleet-Foot Lv 1
Status: OK**

I still had some mana remaining, so I wasn't feeling dizzy just yet. However, I was so exhausted, it felt like it had been four and a half days since my do-over began.

I was accustomed to not having to think about my skills, so it felt physically weird to not have access to them, even though I logically understood they were temporarily unusable.

"Hey, not so fast. You're the leader, right?"

"Gaaaaah!"

Just as one of the delinquents attempted to crawl away, I stabbed the Pyrachnid's Claw of Kindling through his hand, pinning him to the ground.

"Grgaaaagh! It burns! Aaargh!"

"Heh. This is pretty good. It's nice not to get blood all over me," I said nonchalantly as I watched the man scream. My sword continued to burn as it remained lodged in his wound, inflicting excruciating levels of pain that reduced the man to a gibbering wreck.

"When I'm not making fireballs, it doesn't consume too much MP, and the blade is short and easy to handle. It even stops people from dying of blood loss. I'd only ever used it to start fires, but I'm beginning to think this soul blade will be very helpful."

"You...you monster..."

"Agh... Aaaaah..."

I smiled, and the hobbled delinquents' faces filled with despair. The crotches of their pants began to trickle.

"Geez, what a horrible sight. I get no pleasure from this, you know."

I swore revenge on those who betrayed me, and it was those whom I wished to make suffer. Torturing these guys wasn't enough to even get my pulse racing.

"I'm done here. See you."

I took up the Pyrachnid's Claw of Kindling and went around

beheading them. Each swing of my sword was followed by the smell of burning flesh and a soft *thud*.

"I should get going," I said to myself.

I left behind a littered mess of incomplete bodies, unidentifiable feet, and decapitated heads frozen in masks of pure terror.

The man ran without looking back. His gait was floundering; he was only concerned with moving his body forward at any cost. He didn't care about the cuts and scratches he took as he narrowly avoided walls and stray pieces of wood. He was mad with terror, and his instincts were telling him only one thing: *Run. Run for your life.*

Shit, shit, shit, shit, shit!!

Breathless, his body pleaded with him for rest, but his brain drove him relentlessly on. His mind drifted back to the source of his fear.

The day had begun like any other, with the man undertaking some routine work. The people in the slums were those who couldn't show their faces elsewhere. Fugitives, orphans, nobles cast out of their families, merchants whose business ventures had failed, adventurers unable to pay their debts, and even ordinary people simply living in poverty. It was a place filled with shady sorts of every kind.

But it was a necessary evil. Without a slum, all *those* people would spill out into the rest of the city, disrupting the flow of things. Long ago, there was a prosperous trading city that had tried to expel people from the slums by force. While it had succeeded, public order suffered so greatly that merchants avoided the place, sending it on a sharp path down into decline, from which it never recovered. These days, most cities allowed their slums to develop, at least to a certain extent. That way, the citizens could expect a greater quality of everyday life, so long as they didn't accidentally stumble into the slum itself.

However, the inhabitants of the slums were still not given the same level of recognition as the other citizens, and if they grew brazen enough to meddle in public affairs, the kingdom would have no choice but to respond with force.

The slums, for their part, also preferred not to have the city get involved, which was why in any similar settlement, the people who stood at the top took care of its management. They made sure that the slum didn't grow too large, maintained a certain level of order, and ensured that things went as smoothly as possible with the outside world. And so it came to be established that those living in the slum would be responsible for anyone making trouble in the nicer parts of the city. In return, the kingdom would turn a blind eye to what went on inside. In this world, slums were places ruled by no laws of the crown.

The rulers of the slums in the capital had ordered this man, an ex-spy, to keep watch on the entrances to several cities in the area. They needed to know the physical descriptions of anyone entering the city who spelled trouble, and they needed to know about the children of nobles, rich men, or politicians, so that they could protect them if they wandered into a bad part of town. So long as the ex-spy did that, he would be allowed to continue operating outside the law.

The slums were the man's own home, too, and he didn't want to lose them. So when his skill alerted him to a young man heading there from the main streets, he went to his usual vantage point for a better look.

The boy looked to be in his late teens. Dark hair, light build. He was dressed in high-quality, jet-black clothes, but the design was of nothing the man had ever seen, even here in the capital. The boy certainly wasn't a politician's son, but he didn't look like a beggar or an escaped criminal, either. Perhaps he was a noble or a merchant from some faraway town. It was hard to tell how much influence he might have, but he was certainly one to keep an eye on; the man could tell that much.

"In which case, perhaps I should let them rough him up a little before I intervene…," the man muttered to himself as he watched the delinquents slowly surround the boy. He'd step in once the lost boy was wounded.

The man had an agreement with the delinquents. It was a con. If the man decided that it would be bad if the intruder died, he would step in, make a big show of fighting the delinquents off, and earn the person's trust. Then he could gently encourage the stranger to leave without stirring up too much ill will.

He watched as the delinquents raised their fists. *A couple of broken bones should be enough*, he thought as he readied himself to jump in and earn the boy's favor. But what he saw next struck him dumb.

"Huh? Hraaaaaarghhh!"

There was an inhuman scream. The man hurriedly tried to make sense of what he just witnessed, and it was only because of his training as a spy that he was even falteringly able to process the scene. The delinquents launched an attack, and the next second, they were sprawled on the ground. Now the boy was humming to himself, totally unfazed as he unleashed a scene of brutal carnage. At some point—the man didn't see when—a dagger or throwing knife of some sort had appeared in the boy's hand, and when at last the boy pinned the leader of the delinquents to the ground, took up his sword, and executed him, the former spy turned tail and fled as fast as he could.

What could he do against such strength? Would even the royal knight order stand a chance? The boy had a disregard for life like no one he had ever seen outside the slums. He killed those men like it was nothing, like he was doing a job. The work of the reaper.

The man didn't know if the delinquents had blabbed about his involvement, but he did know that if that *thing* set its sights on him, he was as good as dead. So he ran. Anything to get even one step farther away from that monster. His survival instincts were in overdrive, spurring him on over shady bridges toward his destination. He knew there was nothing he could do alone, and so he pressed on, fueled by terror, to find the people in charge of this slum and report what he had seen to them.

Eventually, he arrived at the marketplace. The rows of decaying stalls, a far cry from the neat storefronts of the main streets, dealt in junk and poor-quality trinkets. Slipping past them, he rounded a corner, entered an unimpressive building, and came to a steel door that was flanked by a pair of gargoyles. Two sets of glowing red eyes, equally cold as their gray stone skin, peered down at him.

""Password?""

"Hah...hah... A battered key opens many doors."

""You may enter.""

The man caught his breath and pushed open the steel door. Through the entrance was a different world, a room so clean that it was hard to believe that the slums were still outside its walls. It was filled with many sumptuous fittings, so splendid that it equaled the mansion of any aristocrat elsewhere in the city. Former knights and mercenaries sat around on high-class leather sofas, relaxing and placing bets.

"Hmm? What's up, Jack? You look like you've seen a ghost," noted one.

"Hold on, let me guess," said another. "You ate some dodgy grub, and your guts are about to give up on you. Is that it?"

"Hey, don't think I didn't see that just now! Tryin' to distract me from the game, eh?!"

"*Tsk*, can never pull one over on you…"

Upon seeing his good friends making merry and calling his name, Jack felt his fear settle down. He was safe now, and he could let his guard down.

"I need to see the boss. It's urgent," he announced.

He had to report this incident as soon as possible. Jack didn't know what the boy's motives were, but he knew he wasn't dealing with some kid who got lost and ended up on the wrong side of town. The boy knew about the criminal underworld; that was for sure. His deductions told him that the young man had no influence, but his instincts as a spy told him that the slum would be in great danger if this boy was left at large.

"What's up? Has the crown dispatched troops?"

"…No. I'll tell you later."

There was no way he could sum up the destruction he had witnessed. As a spy, he had learned that it was best not to give only one word when a hundred would suffice. The best way to avoid misunderstandings was to be very clear about things. Thus, he said nothing until he could provide a full description.

He ascended a creaky wooden flight of stairs and knocked on a door at the end of the hallway.

"Who is it?" came a voice.

"It's Jack," he replied. "Boss, I have an urgent report."

"Come in. Door's unlocked."

"Excuse me."

He entered the room with grace and stood before a man about thirty years of age wearing a monocle, with slicked-back white hair.

His narrow eyes gave him the impression of being very wise, and he was scrutinizing a document in his hands.

"You don't mind if I read as you talk?" he asked.

"Of course not, boss."

It wasn't because Jack devalued the importance of his information but because he trusted his boss's ability to listen carefully while also reading.

"Hmm, this may take a while, I see. Take a seat." The boss grew more serious, sensing the gravity in Jack's voice.

"Thank you."

As Jack sat down, his mind raced with where to start. He quickly got his thoughts in order and opened his mouth, but before he could say anything, the boss spoke.

"Hmm, Jack, it appears you screwed up."

Jack faltered, thrown off by his boss's sudden remark.

"Huh? Um, sir, what do you...?"

"Hello, you the boss around here?"

Before he could finish, there was a loud *bang* as the door was *kicked down*. Jack whipped around and almost felt like he could hear the blood drain out of his face. There in the doorway stood the black-haired young man, smiling as though showing up at a friend's place. He held the severed head of a gargoyle in one hand and dragged the mangled body of one of Jack's associates with the other.

Then, noticing Jack, he added, "Oh, thanks for showing me the way. Now we're even for *that little stunt* you pulled on me."

The man ran ahead of me, and I followed. I knew he had a deal with those delinquents who attacked me. I even knew all the details.

That was because they pulled the same trick on me last time, and I got them to spill the whole thing. So I knew where he was hiding, imagined he might try to report to Four-Eyes, who ran this place, and figured I'd have him lead me right there.

I remembered where I met the slum leader the first time, but I had no guarantee that he'd still be in the same place. He used a magic item that allowed him to move his base around and keep his enemies guessing, a prudent measure for one in his position.

I checked my status as I tailed the man and saw I had gained "Track Lv 2" and "Stealth Lv 1." It was proving to be easier to learn and improve skills than it had been the first time around. Even though the levels were reset, I hadn't forgotten how to use the skills. Perhaps it wouldn't take as long as I thought to get back on form.

As I pondered this, I realized that the man had led me straight to his hideout. I was a little surprised. He was good at gathering information, and last time, he had turned out to be a useful ally. He had even once worked as a spy for some foreign country, so he was normally quite a wary person. His folly was that he was also a coward and ran at the first sign of danger, so even though I had never set my sights on him personally, watching those delinquents get slaughtered must have triggered something in him.

Murder was an everyday occurrence in the slums. A man would break your neck for a slice of bread. People died fighting over spoiled apples. Some even killed just for the thrill of it, before the slum leaders found them and beat them to death. Rarely did a day go by in the slums without somebody dying, and I had already seen several people squabbling over food scraps on my way here.

So the man was used to death, especially considering his previous job. He ran because he knew if I spotted him, he would be my next victim. Last time, that was exactly what happened.

The man ducked into a building, and I watched for a while before heading inside after him. There was a familiar steel door guarded by two gargoyles.

""Password?""

"Ah, right. Forgot about these guys."

I scratched my head. The first time around, I had forced the man to bring me here, so the password hadn't been an issue. I had been going for a more delicate approach this time, but it was starting to look like that wouldn't happen.

The person I intended to meet was not one of my sworn enemies. However, he was certainly not my friend, either. He'd slit his mother's throat if it benefitted him, and he was drawn to people who thought the same way. In fact, he would work with anyone who shared his mercenary attitude, no matter who they were. He never lied, but he was always planning to exploit you in some way, and you never knew exactly how. Give him a good enough reason, and he'd betray you without a second thought. I knew that, and he knew that I knew. We were simply using each other.

Still, I could do much worse in these parts, and he was the best partner I was going to get in a country like this one. Also, I needed him to sell the princess's necklace for me, so there was no point in trying to antagonize him right off the bat.

Allowing yourself to lose your cool with him would be a mistake. He'd see through the bluff, bluster his way to your true intentions, and then auction that information off to anyone willing to pay a pretty penny. Sure, you could outbid them and stop that from happening—*if* you even noticed it was happening, that is.

Furthermore, his alchemist combat skills were almost as sharp as his wits. All in all, he was someone you couldn't let your guard down around.

"Sorry for the sudden request, but do you think you could let me speak to your boss for a bit?"

""Password?""

It seemed the gargoyles were not too keen on making conversation. I thought back to the password I heard when I first came here, over three years ago. I found it hard to believe that Four-Eyes would be so stupid as to keep using the same password, but it was worth a try.

"The Nezrahare scares; its hair flares."

""Incorrect. Begone, interloper.""

"…Damn, I knew I shouldn't have bothered."

The gargoyles beat their stone wings and rose from their plinths, seeking to drive me out now that I was considered an *enemy*. As they opened their mouths to cast a spell, I dashed toward them. Unlike dragon breath, which spread far out in a cone, gargoyle breath attacks were shorter and went in a straight line like a laser beam. Even without my skill levels, I was more than powerful enough to deal with a couple of simulacra that could only follow strict orders.

I weaved past the laser and struck one of the gargoyles. Its body felt unsurprisingly hard, and I knew I couldn't break it with my current stats. Thus, I used my Control Mana skill. I transferred mana out of parts of my body, save my legs and eyes, and concentrated it into my arms to strengthen them temporarily. This technique was reserved for emergencies, since it left the rest of my body weak, but at my level, a direct hit would mean death either way.

I also didn't want to use my soul blades. That Four-Eyes was no doubt watching me right now through these gargoyles, and I could do without giving him more information than he needed. Not to mention, gargoyles were exceedingly resistant, the bane of Fire mages everywhere. The Pyrachnid's Claw would be of little use here.

Control Mana, on the other hand, didn't use MP, because it was just moving mana around within the body. As for the downside, the gargoyles' attacks could kill me regardless, but it didn't matter because there was no way these things were going to hit me.

"Gurgh!"

"Gargh!"

I started with one, broke its wings, crushed its arms, grabbed its legs, and swung it into the ground, smashing its head. I hurled what was left of its body at the other one, and when it stopped moving, I held its head and gouged out the magic gems in its eye sockets that gave the gargoyle its power.

"What?! Who goes there?!"

A man of medium build had apparently heard the racket and come running. He hurriedly drew his sword and pointed it at me. Since it looked like I'd already screwed up settling this matter peacefully, I jabbed my fingers into the gargoyle's hollow eyes and slammed its body into the man. The force caused the stony head to detach from its body.

"Gaaagh!"

My odd attack caught my opponent off guard, and he was unable to raise a defense before the gargoyle's heavy stone body launched him against the wall. He slowly collapsed to the floor, hacking up blood as his broken bones pierced his internal organs. I left him and stepped inside.

"Hammonds, no! You bastard, you'll pay for that!"

A slender man, seeing his fallen comrade, swung his sword at me. I parried with the Pyrachnid's Claw before shattering his kneecaps with the gargoyle head that I had brought with me. As he fell to the ground, I grabbed both his arms and gave a firm kick to his spine, bending his limbs back as well.

"Grgaaagh!"

"Al! You brat, how dare you—!"

This was becoming a bore, so I channeled my mana into a menacing aura to intimidate the rest. They were mostly midlevel adventurers or fallen knights whom Four-Eyes had hired to guard this place—brainless muscleheads with low resistance to magic.

I looked around, but the man I'd been following wasn't there. He was probably reporting to Four-Eyes in his office at the far end of the second floor. I looked down at the slender man, his arms and legs snapped like twigs. Might as well use him for intimidation value. It was too late to play friendly now that I'd forced my way through the gargoyles.

I grabbed him by the scruff of his neck and dragged him up to the second floor, ignoring his cries of pain as he struck each step. At the end of the corridor, I came to a warded, soundproofed door. With both my hands full, I had *no other choice* but to focus all my mana into my foot and blast the door clean off its hinges.

"Hello, you the boss around here?" I asked the man I was ostensibly meeting for the first time.

Staring back at me from within the room was the calm, unreadable gaze of Four-Eyes, as well as the pale-white face of the man who had so *graciously* acted as my guide.

"Oh, thanks for showing me the way," I said. "Now we're even for *that little stunt* you pulled on me."

I looked back at Four-Eyes and smiled my best, business-winning smile. Let the negotiations begin.

"I should let you know," he started, "that door contained several of my finest wards. I'm at a loss for words."

"Sorry about that. I had my hands full with these unruly hounds of yours. It was the only way in."

"I do apologize for that. My name is Jufain Gahl. People consider me somewhat of a leader in these parts. What business might you have with me?"

The man who called himself Jufain Gahl did not appear to be the least bit put off by the gargoyle head or fainted bodyguard in my hands, nor the fact that I had destroyed his wards. He simply offered a gentle smile, as though it were of no consequence to him whatsoever.

I had suspected that this wouldn't be enough to intimidate him, but I had hoped to get a *hint* of a reaction at the least. Frustrated, I let the items I'd been holding drop to the floor.

"Oh, just a little something I was hoping you might take off my hands. As for my name, I'll tell you for fifty gold."

I casually took the necklace from my pocket. When Jufain spotted it, the look in his eyes suddenly changed.

"...Jack. Forget what you saw here and leave."

"H-huh?" The white-faced man babbled like an idiot, unable to parse the meaning in Jufain's words.

"You understand well the dangers of knowing too much, Jack. Leave now, while you still can."

"Y-yes, sir!" Jack shot out of the room like a bullet. After I watched him leave, I turned back to Jufain, ready to make a deal.

"Let's talk business," I resumed. "How much will you pay for this?"

"Do you mind if I take a closer look?"

"Not at all. Go ahead." I placed the necklace on his desk. He picked it up delicately and peered at it from multiple angles, checking each stone one by one, along with the fitting that held them, and the chain that fastened it to the wearer's body. Eventually, he placed it back on the table.

"Remarkable craftsmanship. Beautifully cut stones, with a mithril base and chain. The enchantments are impressive, too. Auto HP Regen, Recovery Boost, Record Illusion, and Self-Damage Repair (Poor). I could pay thirty pieces of gold for such an item."

"...Thirty gold, huh?"

A brief interlude about currency. There were seven types of coin in circulation: copper, large copper, silver, large silver, gold, large gold, and platinum. Each coin was worth ten of the denomination below it. A single silver piece would be worth somewhere in the neighborhood of one thousand Japanese yen, though the value of goods differed from our world, so it was hard to say for sure.

Large-gold and platinum coins were therefore so valuable that it was rare to see them in common use, unless you were a big trading firm or national government. For personal trade, people generally stuck to gold coins and lower.

All this is to say that the thirty gold pieces I was being offered were the equivalent of roughly three million yen. Certainly, if you considered the necklace on its own merits and considered it a mere accessory with a few fancy enchantments, such a price was more than fair...*if* you didn't know the full story behind it.

"...I don't appreciate you playing me for a fool, even if it's just to find out how much I know."

"!"

I glared at him. This time, I didn't allow my threatening aura to spread out in all directions, but instead, I focused it directly on the man before me.

"Listen. I'm here because I know you've got the skills I need. So let's skip the pleasantries. Otherwise, I'll have to kill you."

Both he and I knew the score. This was no ordinary necklace. There was an engraving underneath the stones that proved that it belonged to the royal family. In accordance with an ancient oath their ancestors once swore, bestowing the mark required an offering of royal blood and validated the necklace's authenticity while also ensuring that only the royal family could benefit from its effects.

This man surely knew all that, because he had sent Jack away so that the underling couldn't screw anything up. The only reason Jufain would offer me such a low price, then, was that he was trying to gauge my reaction, see how much I knew, and then use that information to gain the upper hand in the negotiations.

…However, he didn't know what this deal meant to me. It wasn't about the money. If it was, I could sell it to anyone and have more than enough to tide me over. This was all part of my plan for revenge. I brought it here because this man could do what I needed. He could return it to its owner in the most delectable manner possible. I was here because I wanted him to serve as my messenger pigeon.

So, just for a second, I set free my domineering aura. One that said, *Don't you dare get in my way.* Jufain took a single breath, which was all it took to recompose himself.

"I do apologize. All I need to know is that the item is indeed genuine, and I can handle that much myself. Any further information, it seems, would cost me quite dearly."

He chuckled softly to himself as he removed his monocle and polished it with a small piece of cloth.

"Let us call it three hundred fifty pieces of gold. I can pay ten up front, but it will take me a while to prepare such a large sum. Return here tomorrow, and you shall have the rest. I will return this to you for now."

"You sure? Not worried I'll take the money and run?"

"If you did, then that would mean I had misjudged you. I would only have myself to blame. Here," he said, placing a small sack of money on the table.

"Thanks." I picked up the sack, opened it, and tossed one of the coins back to Jufain.

"Whatever might this be?"

"What do you mean? It's payment for all the stuff I broke. See you tomorrow." I twisted the corners of my mouth up into a smile. "What, did you *misjudge* me after all?"

"...Fifty gold pieces, was it, to learn your name?"

"Sorry, that offer's gone. You snooze, you lose."

I returned the sack containing nine gold pieces to my pocket and left the room.

"...Heh-heh-heh. I never tire of this slum. You never know what'll happen next."

Jufain was left with a joyful grin on his face. Then he dispelled the disguise he had placed on the gold coin in his hand, reverting it to its original grotesque form—which wriggled and squirmed between his fingers like slime.

Things had gone well, and I was heading back to the city center in good spirits. I half expected to get dragged into another fight, but I made it onto the main road out of the slums without incident. The sun was lower now, and it wouldn't be long before it set completely. I needed to start looking for somewhere to spend the night. I was used to sleeping in wet, stagnant air, on gravel floors whose cold stones stole the heat from my body. It was no surprise that I found myself looking forward to sleeping on my first proper bed in over three months.

"Hold on, this isn't going to work."

A single silver coin was more than enough to secure a room for the night. Prices in general were lower compared with Japan, but the rooms were relatively small, and they didn't serve breakfast. It was quite likely they wouldn't be able to give me change if I tried to pay with a gold coin, and I couldn't go to a more upscale inn where that wouldn't be an issue because those required proof of identity.

Ideally, I wanted to have a good stock of large silvers, silvers, and large coppers, so I scanned my surroundings, trying to locate a money-exchange service. A decent, aboveboard one in the city center might charge less in fees, but for dealing in gold coins and above, they would likely require proof of ID, too. As a result, I looked for one in the slums, where the prices might be higher, but they would *conveniently* neglect to ask such things.

"That one'll do." I picked a place more or less at random and headed over.

"Hey, kid. Looking to make an exchange?" the man whispered.

The word *meathead* was made for this guy. Setting up a money-changing booth in the slums was just asking to be robbed, so the only people who did it either had the backing of a powerful organization or were strong enough to defend it, like he clearly was.

"Yeah, I need to change my gold."

"Gold, huh? How many?"

"Just one for now. I'd like it in silvers and large coppers."

The man took out a pair of scales. On one side, he placed my gold coin, and on the other, a series of small weights.

"Okay, looks genuine. Minus my fee, I can give you five large silvers, twenty-three silvers, and twenty large coppers."

Which meant he was taking a twenty-five-silver fee.

"That's expensive."

"Well, you're free to go elsewhere if you don't like it. Doesn't matter to me."

The fee was a little high, but not outside what one might expect to find in the slums. I also needed to move on and locate an inn. As I thought silently, the man counted out the coins and placed them in a pile before me.

Suddenly, something felt not quite right. Was he going to attack me? No...but something fishy was going on. My hunches had served me well today. I looked more carefully, trying to discern specifically what he was trying to do. However, even now, I could discover nothing strange about him. It was easy to dismiss my feeling, but the irrational part of me still distrusted the man, and my fear was warranted when I took the coins.

"Ah," I said, "I see now. Hey, you."

"Hmm? What's—? Urk!"

I caught the man totally off guard, grabbing him by the neck and pinning him to the back wall.

"You bastard...," he struggled to say. "I gave you the coins, didn't I?"

"Coins? You mean *these coppers*?"

"Wha—?!"

I channeled a bit of mana into the coins, and with a *pop*, the illusion on them disappeared, leaving nothing but dirty coppers. I'd lost my "Sense Magic" skill, as well as the soul blade that gave me a passive buff to perception skills, which meant I'd been unaware of the illusion on the coins until I actually touched them. With some stroke of luck, I noticed it in the end, but I still considered this a failure on my part.

"Heh. It's eat or be eaten here in the slums! *Force Up!*"

Giving up the charade, the man twisted his face into a wicked smile as he cast a spell to raise his physical ability. It seemed he was more intelligence-focused than I had given him credit for.

"For crying out loud, why does every single person I run into have to be like this? This world sucks."

It was really getting on my nerves. My good mood was spoiled, I had to look at this guy's dumb face, but worst of all...

...was the fact that he saw me as such an easy mark.

It made me feel like nothing at all had happened in the last four years, like I was still the same naive idiot I had been the first time around—making all the same mistakes, falling for all the same tricks, and being duped by the same traitors, who even now made my heart burn with the thought of tearing them limb from limb.

"Argh, it makes me sick." I squeezed the man's neck even harder.

"Gaaaargh! Why won't this thing come off?!" he cried, pulling at my arm, but I had already channeled all my mana into it. His Force Up spell wasn't enough for him to take on a member of the royal knight order, let alone me.

"Gah! Grugh! Wh-why...?"

The man struggled to understand why his bulging muscles didn't let him tear off my slender arm with ease. That was because most people didn't know about the technique I used to move mana around my body.

"Listen, I've had a good day so far, so I'm willing to let you go."

"Guh! Ghgh! Gegh!"

A smile appeared on my lips as I thought about my accomplishments today, and I released my grip. The man seemed to finally realize he had messed with someone he didn't want to mess with.

"Y-you want me to apologize?" he asked, the blood gone from his face. "I'm sorry, I shouldn't have done that. I'm begging you, please forgive me!"

"Save your apology. I need you to make up for what you did."

Placing the copper coins into my pocket, I silently drew the Pyrachnid's Claw of Kindling. It was really coming in handy today.

"W-wait! No!"

The usual punishment for counterfeiting was the loss of both hands, along with a large fine. Forging a nation's issued currency was a big deal, after all. Without their hands, a criminal would be unable to pay back the debt incurred by the fine and left with no resort but to commit suicide or sell themselves into slavery.

Thinking this, the man began to scream in panic.

"Don't worry, this sword is way too short to cut off your hands."

I laughed, though in truth, it could do just that. "But it does have some interesting properties. Usually, it's only useful for starting fires or cooking meat, but against certain materials, it can be oddly effective. I wonder if that's because of the monster it came from."

"H-huh?"

To unlock the Pyrachnid's Claw of Kindling, I had to defeat a monster known as the Solar Spider. This creature lived within the pyroducts created by molten lava flowing beneath the surface, and contrary to its appearance, it didn't hunt living things. Its diet consisted instead of the minerals found in those caves, and it used a special excretion called flamevenom to melt down the rocks for consumption.

"Let's see, the punishment ought to fit the crime, don't you think? So let's see that lying mouth of yours finish every last bite," I growled, breaking the man's arms and legs so he couldn't flee.

"Grh! Grrrghaaargh!"

His scream rang throughout the slum, but the man's nightmare was only just beginning.

"Here's the first one. Eat up."

I grabbed a nearby piece of iron and forced it into his mouth, propping it open. Then I took one of the copper coins and placed it onto the Pyrachnid's Claw while running my mana through the soul blade. The coin melted instantly, and I let the molten copper trickle down the blade.

"Graaaaaaaaghhh!"

The droplets gave off a dull gleam as they fell into the man's open mouth, searing his flesh from the inside. However, he didn't die. Flamevenom was hot, but not hot enough to melt rock. Instead, it lowered its target's melting point until it could. The Pyrachnid's Claw was the same. The molten copper was only about three hundred degrees Celsius. Provided I didn't go overboard, he would survive.

"Here comes number two. Just forty-six more to go. It's not so bad with your Force Up on, is it? Okay, here's number three."

Each time I dropped the liquid metal into the man's throat, I smiled as he let out a soundless scream.

By the time the meathead money changer finished imbibing the molten coins, the surroundings were bathed in the red glow of dusk. Another hour, and the sun would dip below the horizon completely. The man had passed out after being forced to eat the last coin. Now he just twitched and spasmed at my feet.

He had kept Force Up going until the very end, and if I just left him there, there was always the chance, however small, that someone would show up and be kind enough to go out of their way and get him medical treatment.

"Hmm, I suppose it wouldn't be very nice of me to just put him out of his misery."

The man reminded me of the pain of being tricked and betrayed. However, I said I'd call it quits if he ate all the coins, and I intended to keep my promise. If I went back on my word just to satisfy my own desires, that'd make me no better than the ones who betrayed me.

He would be no further impediment to my plans for revenge. He had settled his debt, so anything more would no longer be for the sake of retribution. I was an avenger, not some homicidal maniac. If I started deriving pleasure from killing, then I would die before ever getting my revenge and be replaced with something else.

I couldn't allow that to happen. I had sworn vengeance. It was important not to cross the line. This man was not the one who needed to face my wrath. I had a second chance to get back at those who wronged me, and I would not let it go to waste.

"Still, humans are tougher to kill than I expected."

To be honest, I wasn't entirely sure he was going to survive to the end, but the meathead had been tough. I thought he would perish around the twentieth molten coin or so.

The idea had also been to make an *example* of him and strike some fear into anyone else who might cross me. In that sense, leaving him alive could send the message that I was a little too lenient on my foes, especially here in the slums.

That said, I wasn't about to waste my precious healing on him, and if the slum dwellers staring out at us from their hiding spots were to swarm his body like ants once I was gone, that was no business of mine. I forgave him because it was what I said I would do, and there was nothing more to it than that. In the end, I didn't care if he lived or died. He was just another inhabitant of this damn world. I had no duty to help him.

Now that his illusion had been broken, I went to the money changer's stores and picked out five large silvers, twenty-three silvers, and twenty large coppers, then stowed them in my purse along with the gold coins that were already there. I placed the now-bulging sack into my pocket and started walking, without the slightest concern for the man I left behind me.

"Let's see."

I was at the edge of town, a couple of streets off from the city center, in a room in an inn I had picked on a whim. I bent down and placed the cases I was holding under my arms on the floor. The glass bottles inside contained a blue liquid and rattled as I set them down. On my way over, I'd visited an item shop and spent four of my large-silver coins on a couple dozen low-level MP-recovery potions.

"First, let's look at my status. There's something I want to check."

There were three ways of improving your stats in this world. First, you could raise your base stats through training and exercise. Exercise increased your physical stats such as Strength, Dexterity, and Vitality, while using up all your mana every day increased your capacity for magic. However, while these increases weren't negligible, they weren't that high, either. Training eventually gave diminishing returns, and there were also caps depending on your race or species. The reason a dragon was so powerful even at low levels was because of their racial modifiers.

Second, you could gain stat modifiers through skills. Barring a few exceptions, skills came in two types: active skills, which you could perform on demand; and passive skills, which were always on. Some passive skills provided boosts to certain stats, like the uncreatively named "Strength Boost" and "Vitality Boost" skills. Besides these, "HP Recovery Boost" also increased one's max HP, and "MP Consumption Drop" provided an additional Resistance buff.

Incidentally, active skills, such as Air Step and Fleet-Foot, could be activated simply by paying any HP or MP costs, and by using them repeatedly, you could increase your proficiency and level. However, you couldn't use this same technique to train passive skills, because they couldn't be activated. Instead, passive skills each had their own conditions that you had to meet to level them up. For example, the skill I earned today, Track Lv 2, had the condition *Track a target without them noticing for at least ten minutes*. This skill, by the way, provided a bonus Dexterity boost.

As for my soul blades, they could be considered to have both active and passive skills. When using them as a weapon, they had special abilities that were not unlike active skills, and like passive skills, soul blades were unlocked by performing certain feats and provided bonuses to your stats once you owned them.

To take my Nephrite Blade of Verdure as an example, it provided modifiers to Stamina, Vitality, and Resistance, while the Pyrachnid's

Claw of Kindling boosted Dexterity and Vitality. However, soul-blade modifiers were additive—increasing your stats by fifty, for example—while skills were multiplicative, applying a percentage increase. Therefore, as my level increased and my base stats went up, the modifiers from my passive skills would become more significant.

But I digress. The third way of increasing your stats was through levels. Like training, this raised your stats' base values, but the payoff was far greater. The only way to increase your level was to amass experience, which was given from killing a "living thing or object with a will of its own," according to the status screen. Of course, that included humans. The stronger they were, the more experience you gained.

There was one more part to this stat-modifier business, but it was not widely known, and those who did know had their reasons for keeping it a secret. I'll touch on that some other time.

I hadn't finished off the bodyguards in Jufain's residence, so assuming their friends had healing potions on hand, they should still be alive. Other than that, I had killed six delinquents and two gargoyles so far.

"...Hmm, but I'm still level one. Why?"

The delinquents were one thing. Their levels were unexpectedly low, and with all my stat bonuses, I was far stronger than them. It was no surprise that they hadn't given me enough experience to level up, but the gargoyles had higher stats than me. Why else would my unfortified punch have no effect? Something was not right here. I tapped on the word *Level*.

STATUS

Current Level: 1

Experience: −20,000/150

Experience Remaining: 1,012

- -

Allocate Remaining Experience.

Remaining: 1,012

[000000] OK / CANCEL

- -

[Soul Blade of Beginnings ▽]

[Pyrachnid's Claw of Kindling ▽]

[Nephrite Blade of Verdure ▽]

[Tailor's Hook of Mending ▽]

[Holy Sword of Retribution ▽]

A window appeared, and when I read it, I dipped my head and pinched the bridge of my nose.

"Oh, Goddess of Earth," I grumbled under my breath. "I know you said levels were deducted based on the time I spent alive, but I didn't think you meant it could go negative!"

I gave a brief sigh and tried to focus. The *Current Level* and *Experience* fields were ones I had seen before, but this *Experience Remaining* was new to me. The name gave me some clues as to its function, but to make sure, I gave it a tap.

"I knew it..."

A scrollable dial wheel appeared when I touched the numeric entry field, allowing me to allocate my experience points. Presumably, this was because I now needed to pay experience to reunlock my soul blades.

In any case, it was clear that my level would not be going up without some serious grinding. It was the difference in stats that mattered when determining gained experience from an enemy, not level, and since my stats were being boosted by my soul blades, I wouldn't be getting a lot of experience unless it was from some *juicy* prey like those gargoyles.

I closed the tab and took a look at my soul blades instead. Glancing at the list, I noticed there was one other usable blade.

"So the ones I can use right now are the Soul Blade of Beginnings, the Pyrachnid's Claw of Kindling, the Nephrite Blade of Verdure, the Tailor's Hook of Mending, and the Holy Sword of Retribution."

The other soul blades each indicated that they cost at least three thousand experience points to unlock, and the ones I wanted first were even higher than that. I didn't have to think about that just yet, though. First, I investigated the soul blades I had currently, since it seemed they would be my main weapons for a while.

"Hmm, the Holy Sword of Retribution. I see..."

It turned out that this had been the source of my extraordinarily canny hunches of late. This sword provided a passive boon that warned me of any evil intentions directed my way. I noticed several other abilities as I scanned the page. Then there, at the bottom, were a list of its unlock conditions.

1. Sincerely swear revenge against at least ten people you once trusted.
2. Total amount of damage received from those people exceeds a certain threshold.

I must have unlocked this sword just before I died.

"Come to think of it, I wonder what happened to..."

After I had more or less digested its abilities, I took another look at the soul-blade list and scrolled down to the very bottom. There was one entry there whose name was simply ??????????

It had appeared sometime after I slew the demon lord, though I never noticed exactly when, and it was still here now, the second time around. Nothing happened when I tapped on it, either, and unlike the other soul blades, there was no way to unlock it using experience points. It didn't even have the lock icon. As far as I could tell, it would just remain grayed out forever.

"Not much to be happy about, is there...?"

With my current stats, I could only defeat around seventy royal knights before giving up the ghost. While it would take too long for me to pay off my entire debt and start leveling up, I could train my skills and start improving my stats immediately. I had no time to waste.

"Then I guess I'll go buy one tomorrow. They'll be useful after I leave the city, too."

I started planning out what I would need after I left the city. Then once I settled my other affairs, I turned my mind toward the night's main event. I placed the necklace on the center of the room's table and readied an MP potion in my left hand. Then with my right, I took the Tailor's Hook of Mending, a sword that had a long, narrow spike for a blade and a tip that was bent like a bird's talon.

"Man, it sure is a shame I won't get to see this. Hmm, perhaps I could get that Four-Eyes to capture some images for me?"

This dastardly plan was nothing more than a *slight* inconvenience in the grand scheme of things, but still, I would have loved to see the faces of the princess or her parents when it came to fruition. Maybe it would be worth pulling out all the stops on this one.

Also, I hadn't really spent too much time interacting with the king and queen, so it was hard to say what the best way of getting revenge on them would be. I needed more information on them, no matter how risky it was. So as much as I shuddered to think of indebting myself even more to Four-Eyes, it had to be done. I would lick the dirt off his boots if it helped me get my revenge.

"However... Heh-heh-heh..."

I couldn't help grinning as I thought of my plan going off. It'd been a long day, and I was feeling tired, but my work wasn't over yet. If I didn't do this, I wouldn't be able to sleep.

I channeled my mana into the Tailor's Hook of Mending and hummed a merry tune.

"La-la-la! ♪ La-la! ♪ La-la-la-la! ♪"

It was morning, just as the faint glow of the impending dawn brought the day's first light to the pitch-dark sky. My singing was slightly off tune, but with no less spirit behind it as I grinned maniacally at the fruits of my effort.

"La-la-la! ♪ La-la-la-la! ♪ La-la! ♪"

My grueling work had taken longer than I expected, and in the end, I never got to sleep in the bed I'd dreamed of for the last three months. Instead, I added those frustrations to the revenge pile and continued, guzzling MP potions along the way.

I threw myself into my task, and once the hard part was over, I coasted on a second wind that made me completely forget about the exhaustion of the previous day. The word *sleep* was like a foreign language to me, and I was so far gone that I ended up drinking all my leftover MP potions at once.

I could tell I was losing it, but I relied on the adrenaline pumping through me to get me through the night, and at long last, I held the finished necklace in my hands. Once dawn broke for real, the sunlight would help me calm back down. Until then, I belted out a song they used to play on the radio while I did some stretches.

"SHUT UP! DO YOU HAVE ANY IDEA WHAT TIME IT IS?!"

"Ah... S-sorry..."

An unexpected scream from the room next door brought me back to my senses. I had forgotten what it was like to hole up in a hotel with other people sleeping nearby. Too long spent alone on the run. From across these thin walls, he'd probably heard the song I'd been singing all night as well.

Oh my god. I want to diiiie! How embarrassing!

I dived onto the bed and started rolling around to get the memory out of my mind, when my neighbor slammed on the wall again.

"I SAID SHUT UP!"

I guess I hadn't quite settled down yet. *Sorry, my brain is on strike. I'm really sorry. I hate my life. I'm going to go to bed.*

I was looking forward to a good night's rest, but I didn't want to get too comfortable and oversleep. There were still some things to take care of before leaving the city.

The previous day, the summoning chamber had been under the princess's orders, so any outsiders couldn't step into the place. By now, they would have found her and started administering medical treatment. Those wounds had taken quite some time to inflict, and they should still take a while to heal, but I wanted to be out of this city as soon as possible.

I looked at the bed with a mixture of longing and regret before seating my back to the wall, next to the window, so that the rising sun would be my alarm clock.

I overslept. Like, seriously overslept.

...I mean, come on! I didn't think the sky would cloud over and block the light. What do you mean, I should know everything from the first time around? How am I supposed to remember what the weather was like four years ago?!

By now, the sun was high overhead, and it was already midday. I checked out of the inn as quickly as I could, but my shopping would have to wait until later. For now, I grabbed some lunch at one of the many food stalls before heading once again into the slums.

My *example-making* must have worked, for no delinquents accosted me today, and I arrived promptly at my destination. I passed by the place where I ran into that money changer, but today, he was nowhere to be found, and another one had popped up in his place. When he saw me, his face grew stiff, and he hurriedly bowed his head, and when I smiled back, he turned oddly pale.

I wasn't looking to start a fight or anything, unless he gave me a reason.

Eventually, I came to the gargoyles, which were completely back to normal as if nothing had happened. In fact, if anything, they were a little stronger than before. It was only when I saw them that I remembered I still didn't know the password. As I was wondering what to do, they addressed me in unison.

""You may pass.""

Well, that was convenient. I entered Jufain's base and was met with the icy glares of the hired muscleheads I had run into the previous day.

"I won't cause any trouble if you don't, so settle down, friends," I said with a sigh.

The bodyguards still watched me intensely. An understandable reaction, but one that would do them little good. They might as well relax and save themselves the stress. If they picked a fight with me, they'd be dead either way.

I headed up the stairs to the second floor, where Jufain was waiting for me with a smile. On his desk were four sacks of gold coins. Judging by the sizes, it looked like three bags of a hundred coins and one bag of forty.

"Here is the money we agreed on," he stated. "Would you like to count it?"

"No need," I assured. "Anyone willing to pull cheap tricks wouldn't last long in that chair." Mainly, I just couldn't be bothered, but I figured I'd pay him the compliment. "All right then, here's the necklace."

"Thank you very much. You've given me something quite remarkable. Hmm? ...Ah, I see..."

Jufain clearly realized something as he took the necklace. Drat, and I'd even gone to the trouble of using a high-level disguise, hoping he wouldn't notice. You just couldn't pull one over on him.

"My, you are a handful," he remarked. "I can hardly present this to the royal family in person now, can I?"

"That's rich—as if you would ever do something so risky. Just foist it off on some noble who's been giving you trouble and enjoy watching him take the fall. It's not like you were actually planning to shoulder the risk of directly dealing with the royals. Oh, the shit that comes out of your mouth."

I'd learned the first time around that the king, queen, and princess viewed the slum as a necessary evil at best. When rumors of the demon lord first started to circulate, people bought up goods, driving up prices, and the slum began to grow. It was obvious that if Jufain went to the king with his prized jewels in hand, the king would call them thieves and have the entire slum thrown in chains, forced to work as slaves for the good of the kingdom until they drew their last breaths. In fact, I learned later that he'd tried something just like that, and the people almost rebelled against him for it. After I defeated the demon lord and outlasted my usefulness, he jumped on the opportunity and claimed *I* had been the one to order their enslavement, which was what landed me in such hot water. Knowing him, it was almost certain he'd try to pull the same trick again, even if someone else had to be his scapegoat this time.

"Okay," I said, "I admit I've ruined your chances to buddy up with a powerful nobleman. How about I pay you twenty gold to make up for it, and another twenty if you do me a small favor?"

"I have no reason to accept either of those. I would much rather know how you modified this item so greatly in just a single night."

"Sorry, that's a trade secret. So will you do it or not?"

"I can't answer until I know what the favor is," replied Jufain, giving a light shrug.

"Fair enough," I replied. "Don't worry, it's not too difficult. I just want you to make one of those alchemical life-forms for me. You know, the one you tried to spy on me with. I want it to record something in the castle and bring it back to me, maybe by turning into a bird or something."

"I will be the one who pays the price if they find out where it came from. It'll have to be eighty gold."

"And? Surely, that's no problem for someone of your skills. Thirty gold."

"You misunderstand. Whether or not I *can* do it is not the issue. The penalty for failure simply outweighs the benefit. Seventy gold."

"Come on. I bet the nobles' estates are filled with your monitoring devices. All I'm asking is that you add the castle to that. Fifty gold."

"Spying on the nobility and spying on the king are in two completely different levels of risk. Sixty gold. Ahhh, I see the sky is finally clearing up."

Throughout the negotiations, Jufain had not once broken my gaze, but upon saying this, he smiled and turned to look out the window. It was his way of saying to take it or leave it.

"...Fine, it's a deal," I grumbled. "You really are the stingiest bastard I've ever had the displeasure of dealing with."

"Flattery will get you nowhere. A pleasure doing business with you."

Then Jufain opened one of the sacks and counted out precisely forty gold coins, transferring them one by one into a second bag on his desk. He then took it along with the smaller bag containing the last forty gold coins of my payment to make up eighty coins—consisting of the twenty I was offering for pulling that trick over him, plus the sixty we had just agreed on. Finally, he cleared away those two sacks and placed an object on the desk. It was a small glass bottle filled with a golden, metallic liquid.

"Here you are. The receiver to my Peeping Eye. If all goes well, this should give you a view of what the transmitter sees when it activates."

I picked up the sealed bottle and placed it in my bag. "Now, why do you just so *happen* to have the thing I needed on hand, I wonder...?"

"That's a trade secret," replied Jufain with a disturbingly perfect fake smile.

"Well, catch you later, though I hope we never meet again," I mentioned. I knew it was too much to wish for.

"Oh, don't be that way. I, for one, will welcome you back here at any time."

It was never easy to tell how serious he was being. I couldn't think of anything to say to wipe the grin off his face, so I left without another word. Somehow, it felt like I had just lost.

Well, if nothing else, I had little to worry about with Jufain's alchemy on my side. Now I just had to hope there was no one at the castle whose senses rivaled his. In all the time I knew the princess, I never once saw her take that necklace off. Perhaps there was some practical or sentimental reason there, but either way, I wouldn't be surprised if she put it on immediately without even checking it first.

And when she did…

"Hee-hee-hee! I can't wait to see the look on her face!"

It had been another good day, and I was in another good mood. It was a feeling I hadn't felt in over a year. A year of life on the run, thinking only about my next meal or what dangers lay around me, without a single moment to relax. I practically skipped through the slum, euphoric as I imagined the princess's face contorted with pain and the horrified looks on the faces of her dear mother and father. Once again, I gave thanks for being granted a second chance.

"Ahhh, how nice it is to have things to look forward to again!"

After leaving Jufain's base, I set out once again toward the edge of the slums. The previous day, I had been meaning to get a little shopping done with my advance payment, but now that I had the whole sum, it was probably best to get the big purchase out of the way first. For safety, I stowed my gold sacks into a large drawstring bag that was commonly used in this world to hold supplies for long journeys on foot. After that, I headed to a lesser-traveled area of the slum. Here, adventurers walked the streets, while workers from who-knew-where hid their faces with filthy rags. This was the one place in the slums where buyers didn't have to acknowledge the poor. A place to deal in all sorts of illicit goods. The black market. You could find forbidden tomes, drugs, fenced goods, dangerous ingredients, and, of course, slaves.

Some were prisoners of war or convicts forced to work in the country's mines. Others were ruined by debt or kidnapped, then bought and sold as property.

As a slave, it was hard to know how you'd be treated. It depended on the master. However, very few slave owners considered their slaves to be disposable. If nothing else, they were expensive products.

There were even sellers who proudly set up shop in the city center and were frequented by nobility and other wealthy individuals, with many high-quality slaves for sale. However, without the proper connections, it was impossible to visit these particular sellers. Those without friends in high places, or who were willing to settle for lower-quality products at cheaper prices, came here.

I wandered the market, trying to recall its layout from the last time I was here. Wherever I went, well-informed violent types went scurrying off into dark corners when they laid eyes on me.

"I had meant to make an example...but maybe I took things too far?"

Word traveled fast. It turned out the mage I'd humiliated was a fairly influential troublemaker. By beating him so thoroughly, I'd made quite the impression in this might-ruled society.

"Oh well. At least it means no one will bug me anymore."

I was looking for a place where I could do business as inconspicuously as possible, and as soon as I finished my train of thought, I came across a shop that looked relatively empty. Inside, there were no other customers but me. Perfect. The idle shopkeeper looked me up and down and, upon realizing I was nobody of importance, addressed me plainly.

"Come to buy slaves, have you? What's yer budget?"

I considered how much money I might need to take care of the rest of my business, then replied:

"I'm looking to get a single slave for about ten gold. Bring some out for me, and I'll take my pick."

Apparently, at the fancier slave markets, the clientele would often pay in large-gold coins and sometimes even platinum if the *goods* were of high enough quality. Here in the slums, you never knew what you were going to find, but even the cheapest slave would set you back three gold coins or so. Seven or eight gold was more common, so a budget of ten gold should cover all but the most expensive.

"Pardon me fer asking, but have you got the cash?"

The shopkeeper tossed me a suspicious look. A nobleman's son would go upmarket, and I looked too weak to be an adventurer. A young Japanese man like me probably appeared little more to him than a kid, unlikely to have that kind of money on him.

However, it made me angry to be looked down on, even if I understood where he was coming from.

"...See for yourself," I growled as threateningly as possible, placing a bag of coins onto the counter.

"Oh...oh, no, that's quite all right! Please come this way, sir!"

The man's complete change of heart annoyed me. It reminded me of the two-faced traitors I hated with such a passion. Unfortunately, venting my anger on him would do nothing to get back at them, so instead, I held my tongue and followed him into the back rooms.

There sat slaves in iron cages, wrists and ankles bound in chains, their eyes consumed by darkness. There was no concept of nutritional science or good hygiene in this world, but even by the denizens' standards, the environment in these halls was bleak.

There were two reasons I was buying a slave. The first was for disguise. After all, if the kingdom came after me, they would only be looking for a single young man with black hair and strange clothes.

Second, I needed a training partner. There were many skills that were impossible to acquire and train if you were alone, and even though I could use the Holy Sword of Retribution to detect if someone would betray me, I had not the slightest intention of making any friends, either. Hence, I needed a slave. Just until my skills were ready, then I could pay them off and cut them loose, and if worse came to worst and they continued to get in my way, I could always deal with them *permanently*.

Still, it made me sick to my stomach to treat anyone the way I was treated, to dispose of them after they'd served their usefulness, even if that person was a slave. As such, I wouldn't have to go that far unless they actually turned against me. Also, as I honed my own skills against them, the slave's skills would improve as well, so it was safe to assume they'd have the bare minimum they needed to survive if I did end up leaving them on their own.

What I was looking for was a transactional relationship, ideally where I could get as much out of it as I put in. That was what I thought...

...until I saw the eyes of a certain slave.

"As you can see, this slave is in prime working condition. *The one over there* would cost you a pretty penny more, but here..."

"Hey. Who's the one at the far end?"

"Hmm? Ah, the *Lagonid* girl, you mean. Truth be told, I was planning on disposing of her. I brought her here to the capital because I heard the noblemen in these parts were into that sort of thing, but

I've been having trouble finding a buyer. She looks sweet on the outside, but that rabbit's got a vicious streak. Even the Slave Brand couldn't persuade her to behave, and she nearly died in the process. A shame. She's got a pretty face, but nobody wants to buy a girl who's willing to kill you during the deed."

Human supremacy was rooted in the religion here in the capital, and beastfolk faced terrible persecution. Hence, it was rare to see one around here, and relations with the beastfolk country, which lay beyond the far side of the empire, were strained. Of course, humans were just as hated over there as beastfolk were here, so the two realms were as bad as each other.

"I've made my decision. I'll take her."

"Huh? I don't think you understand, sir. Those beastfolk are stronger than they appear. She really might murder you in your bedsheets if you're not careful."

"I don't care. I'll pay you ten gold pieces if we can seal the deal immediately."

"Well, if you're sure, sir, then it's fine by me... Is this your first time buying a slave?"

"Yes, it is. Why?"

"In that case, sir, we'll have to set up your Master's Mark."

"My what?"

"Your Master's Mark, sir. It will allow you to control your slaves by inflicting pain upon them at your discretion."

We returned to the front of the store, and I signed the purchase agreement. Then I signed another document that granted me my Master's Mark. This document was itself a magic item, and as soon as I placed my signature, it went up in flames, and a rudimentary magic circle appeared on the back of my hand.

System message: "Master's Lash of Taming" unlocked.

* * *

It appeared I had acquired a new soul blade. I would have to look at that later.

"Now simply hold the Mark above her Slave Brand and activate it using your mana. That will bring the slave under your control."

"Can't another master just overwrite her Brand, then?"

"No. The Slave Brand will change in shape to match your Mark, and any further modifications will be impossible until your contract ends."

He led me back to the cells, to the far end of the room. The iron grate squeaked as he pulled it open, and I stepped inside.

"…"

Like a prisoner, she was bound and gagged, her wrists in chains and large iron balls attached to her ankles. Bruises covered her body from head to toe, and her rags were speckled with blood, possibly her own. Her long hair was not quite orange but dark flaxen, matted and dry, as though it had gone neglected during her long imprisonment. Her distinctive, rabbitlike ears drooped. From the looks of it, she once had quite a fine body, but now she looked emaciated and weak. Her eyes were sullen, and the skin of her arms, legs, and cheeks stretched thin over her bones.

I wondered how long she'd been like this. She looked so tired that simply groaning used up all her energy, and she was caked in dirt, which showed she hadn't seen the inside of a bathtub for a very long time. However…

"Ah, what brilliant eyes," I observed.

Yes, even in her pitiable state, those eyes of hers yet burned.

A dark, dark flame. Like magma, churning deep below the earth.

Any normal person would have given up long ago, when the wounds inflicted on their body became too much to bear. And yet her eyes brimmed with such heat and pressure, they seemed ready to go supernova.

*   *   *

They were the sweet, sweet eyes of revenge.

I stroked her cheek and peered deeply into them. The Holy Sword of Retribution showed me the evils that lurked in other people's hearts, but I didn't need it to detect the lust for revenge she bore. Her eyes shone with a pure and burning hate.

"Don't…touch…me…human."

A pointed glare. A flash of teeth. We were two of a kind, no doubt about it. We were both fated to walk the path of revenge for the rest of our lives—unable to find peace until we exacted our retribution. Just like me, she was possessed of a pitch-dark soul that burned her away from the inside.

"…"

First, I completed the procedure to contract her as my slave. Channeling mana into my hand, I placed it against the Brand on the back of her neck.

"Grh! Aaaaaaaarghhh!"

The Brand glowed with a magical light as the shape that was carved into her flesh transformed. When the light dimmed and her screams of pain subsided, I took out from my bag two potions—one for HP and one for MP, which I used for emergencies—and emptied them both into her mouth.

"Nglg! Glglg! Gluuughhh!"

"Now maybe you're feeling well enough to talk to me," I said.

My appraisal soul blade was still locked, but it was clear that some debilitating condition was impacting all her stats. HP and MP were both tied to Stamina. Restoring them wouldn't bring her stats back to normal, but they should at least give her some energy.

"What…?" she began.

"Who is it you want to kill?"

My words lingered in the silence of the cell. I watched her intently. Through the windows of her eyes, the same color as her hair, I observed the raging darkness within. It was that to which I addressed my question.

"Who do you want revenge on?"

CHAPTER 3
The Beastfolk Girl and
the Tormenting Hunger

There's nothing here to eat…"

"We searched so hard, and not a single bite…"

To the north of the Orollea Kingdom, in a small village just outside the bordering Girigal Empire, a girl who turned fifteen that year was foraging in the snowy woods alongside her friend Lucia.

In those parts, the temperature dropped low in the winter, and though the crops were usually bountiful, the last ten years had seen a steady decline. At times like these, the village sought to endure the season by foraging for nature's bounty in the nearby forests. However, this year, winter had come unusually early and blocked off the forest with snow before the village could secure adequate reserves. Though children were not permitted to enter the forest during this time of the year, the two girls had slipped away from the village while the men were away on hunting expeditions.

Lucia shrank into herself apologetically. Her wavy blond hair fell neatly around her shoulders. "I'm sorry for making you come with me, Minnalis. I just wanted Kril to have something to eat on his birthday…"

"No, it's okay," replied the girl, shaking her head. "Besides, I was the one who said we should search the forest. I wanted to celebrate, too."

The two children had entered the forest, without telling the grown-ups, to find food for their friend to eat. However, even the trees that still had their leaves bore no fruit, and the snow fell so heavily around their roots that it was impossible to turn up even a single blade of wild grass.

Still, the girls searched the forest, their eyes wide with curiosity, looking for the special tree they had heard stories of that yielded exceptional fruit only in the winter. They forged ahead, the snow crunching underfoot as they walked. Before long, they came to the depths of the forest—a place they were told never to enter, even in the warmer months.

"Minnalis... Don't you think we should head back soon?"

"Y-yeah. Let's go home, even though we couldn't find anything."

Hearing Lucia's worried tone, the other girl grew nervous, too, and was relieved to think of the village again. For a while now, the forest had felt darker, more foreboding, though in appearances, nothing about it had changed.

Lucia, who was just a simple child, couldn't tell the difference. But the girl could, for *unbeknownst to the village, she was a beastfolk.* Her heightened senses were many times more sensitive than those of a human. To her, this part of the forest was like a different place entirely, and the eeriness made her skin crawl. She was the one who suggested they search for the fruit in the first place, though, and she couldn't bring herself to suggest turning back when they had still not found it.

"Okay then," she said, facing back where they came from.

"Ah, wait! Minnalis, look over there!" Lucia stopped and pointed at a tree a little way ahead.

It was difficult to get a good look through the branches, but the girl could definitely see several small yellow fruits that were about the size of fists. Lucia beamed as she pointed them out.

"Thank goodness! It wasn't a waste to come all the way out here after all! Let's grab them and head…back…"

Then all the blood drained from Lucia's face. When the other girl saw *it*, she, too, went pale.

"Grrrrrah…!"

It was a single goblin.

Dwarfish in size with a repugnant face and green skin, goblins were known for their excessive breeding rate, and they were considered vermin wherever they sprung up. The girls had seen them before, albeit from a distance, as the creatures often appeared during harvest time to plunder the fields. The men of the village would band together to repel them, or if the monsters' numbers were too great, then adventurers would be hired. One goblin would not be too much for the pair to outrun, even as young as the two girls were. However, the problem was the color of the creature's skin. While normal goblins were green, this one was a deep blue.

"A variant…"

Regular goblins were weak monsters, the kind a novice adventurer might slay while collecting herbs for a quest. They were recommended targets for beginners because of their low threat level, and they were relatively harmless unless you encountered a large group of them. However, on rare occasions, specimens were born that exceeded the capabilities of their species. Goblin Soldiers and Goblin Magicians were famous examples of this phenomenon. However, there were also individuals whose abilities were so far removed that they were like a different species. These were called "variants."

The girl had heard about them once before from a party of adventurers who stopped in the village. The monsters looked almost identical to a regular goblin, except for their dark-blue skin. Unlike their kin, which kept to warm climates and abhorred the cold, these variants thrived in the chilly climate and appeared in snowy areas, though sightings were rare. Their resistance to ice was extremely high, and weak magic would bounce right off them. Their intelligence and abilities, as well as their ferocity, were also several levels higher than those of other goblins.

"An Ice...Goblin...," breathed out the girl.

Lucia, on the other hand, didn't know what it was, but she could feel its overpowering aura all the same. Fortunately, the goblin was engrossed in picking fruit and hadn't noticed the girls.

"Lucia, stay calm. We have to..."

"Nooo! Noooooooo!"

"L-Lucia!"

Before they could quietly make their escape, Lucia succumbed to pure fear. She let out a terrified yell and started running, unable to hear a single word that the other girl was saying.

"No! No! Nooooo!"

"Lucia!"

Lucia was suffering from the Panic status condition, the other girl realized. She had heard about it before when she was listening to the adventurers talking about their experiences, though there was nothing she could do to help her friend now. The girl turned to flee, catching one last sight of the Ice Goblin looking up in their direction and grinning as it spotted a more delicious *meal*.

The girls scrambled through the snow, hoping against hope to make it back to the village in time, but the goblin was clearly closing in on them. Running for her life, Lucia took one step on the unfamiliar, snow-covered paths and fell head over heels.

"Eek!"

"Lucia!"

"Urgh... Ow..."

CHAPTER 3

Lucia had sprained her ankle as she fell into the deep snow, and she was now unable to stand. Even if the girl helped her up, her injury would make it impossible for the two of them to outrun the Ice Goblin.

"Grah-grah-grah-grah!"

The foul creature closed in on Lucia with mocking laughter, but the girl had the power to save her. The goblin was rich in mana, but it couldn't cast spells. If she used her beastfolk strength, she could overpower it. However...

"Remember, Minnalis. You must never use your power in front of others. If you do, the illusion I placed upon you will be dispelled, and your rabbit ears and tail will be revealed."

"Why is that bad, Mom? Why can't people know we're beastfolk?"

"I wish I knew, sweetie. We just look a little different; that's all..."

"No! Nooooo! I don't wanna die! I don't wanna diiiie!"

...I'm sorry, Mom!

Seeing her friend in danger, the girl flew toward the goblin, disregarding the promise she made to her mother.

"Rrraaaaargh!"

"Grah?!"

Her flying kick connected with the goblin's stomach. The force of the attack blasted the small creature away and into a nearby tree. Such a hit would have killed a regular goblin instantly, but the variant Ice Goblin sprung quickly to its feet and, displaying its heightened intellect, deduced that continuing to engage the girl would be a poor idea. Giving the pair a glowering look, it retreated into the depths of the forest.

"Lucia! Are you okay?! Are you hurt?"

"Mi-Minnalis... What are...?"

85

With a trembling finger, Lucia pointed, astonished, at the ears atop the other girl's head.

Different kinds of beastfolk had different strengths and weaknesses, but on the whole, their physical stats were higher than those of humans, as well as their HP and MP. However, their mana was unique in that it grew weaker the farther away it traveled from their bodies, making their ranged attack magic considerably less effective compared with other races. The cloaking magic that hid her ears was a thin layer of illusion that wrapped around the body, so it could get around this weakness.

Her bloodline was particularly skilled at illusion magic, so it was no great hardship to craft a disguise that endured for long periods of time. However, since she'd used her full beastfolk power, the force of the mana emanating from her body blew the illusion away.

"Ah...er... I'm...I'm sorry, Lucia. I'm sorry I never told you. Please keep this a secret!"

"Huh?! Oh, er, okay."

The girl gave a reassuring smile to her friend, who was still reeling from the shock.

The girl was not the child she once was. She knew the contempt this country had for her kind. That was why she'd followed her mother's words all this time and never told a soul about her heritage, not even her closest friend.

"There we go."

The girl recast the illusion that concealed her ears and tail. She learned the spell about four or five years ago. Before that, her mother always did it for her.

"Let's get back to the village. We didn't find any food, but we might run into more monsters, and it's getting dark."

"Yeah...you're right. Let's go home."

*   *   *

It was already evening by the time they arrived back at the village. After the village elder scolded them thoroughly for going into the forest in winter, the two were sent home to await their punishment the next day. The girl went to her mother—Maris, who was bedridden—and told her about what happened in the forest.

"I see. You saved your friend," Maris said with a weak smile.

The girl wondered why her mother seemed so sad, but as she was tired from the day's events and unused to using her full strength, it didn't take long before she fell sound asleep, dreaming sweet dreams of finding all sorts of fruits in the snowbound forest.

The next day, she was awoken by a knock on the door and led to the village square. For some reason, her mother was brought along as well.

"Hmm? What's going on? Isn't this *my* punishment? Why is Mom…?"

She was dragged along to where a large crowd had gathered. She stared, confused, at their thorny glares, and when the village elder spoke, his words caused her mind to go blank.

"Minnalis. Maris. Is it true that you two are beastfolk?"

The girl couldn't believe her ears. She barely understood what she was hearing.

"I'll ask again. Are you two beastfolk?"

The elder's words rang once more in her thoughts.

Why? Why? Why? Why? How did this happen?

Her mind was a storm of questions. She couldn't process this information. She looked up at her mother for help and reassurance. Her mother's countenance was grim, yet with a determined look, she dispelled the illusion that kept her true identity hidden.

A murmur swept through the crowd, and their eyes changed. It was like they were looking upon a pile of exterminated goblins whose bodies had rotted. The faces of the villagers she loved like family were twisted with disgust.

"Mo... Mom..."

The situation was changing too fast for her to keep up. Her confusion kept growing. She looked at the face of the village elder. His eyes were the coldest, most disdainful eyes she had ever seen. They scared her. Scared her even more than the Ice Goblin she had fought the previous day.

"We are beastfolk, as you can see. I'm very sorry for hiding it all this time."

Her mother pressed her head to the cold, hard dirt in apology. Finally, the girl understood. The villagers hated them both.

"So Lucia was telling the truth...," muttered the elder.

"L-Lucia?! No... No, she couldn't have...," the girl stammered. Lucia promised not to tell a soul the previous day. The girl looked around, searching for someone to tell her it was a lie, and there, nestled among the crowd, she saw the faces of her best friends.

Then her hopes of salvation were dashed. The boy, Kril, looked back as if she were garbage. And there, nestled by his side, stood Lucia, grinning, just out of his periphery.

"Wh-why? You said you wouldn't tell anybody!"

The young girl couldn't help but yell.

Lucia clung tightly to Kril's arm as though afraid. "Eek! Kril..."

"Don't worry, Lucia. It's okay," assured Kril, patting her back gently and firing the girl a deadly glare. "Leave Lucia alone! I couldn't believe it at first, but you really are evil! I trusted you!"

"What? What are you...?"

"Don't play dumb! Lucia told me everything! You've been bullying her this whole time and threatening her to keep quiet! You made her cry!"

"Wha...?"

The girl was speechless. Lost for words. Even if she could say them, her mind utterly failed to come up with any words. Then her mother spoke again.

"Elder, I don't care what you do to me, but please—please don't hurt her! Please... I at least want her to live to see her eighteenth birthday..."

Maris lowered her head as she embraced her daughter. She had known this would happen ever since her daughter told her what happened in the forest. She couldn't leave because of her sick health, and she knew her daughter would never run away without her. This was the only thing she could do.

"Please... I beg of you..."

"Foul beastfolk!" One villager had picked up a stone off the ground and hurled it at her.

"Who are you trying to fool?"

"I can't believe you lied to us all this time!"

"Damn animals in human clothing!"

One by one, the villagers joined in, raining down scathing words and sharp rocks upon the pair.

"Please... Please spare my child... Urkh!"

"Mom!"

Among the thrown stones, a large one struck Maris's skull, drawing blood, and the girl instinctively imposed her own body to protect her. In all the confusion, her illusion had come undone, and her ears and tail were fully visible. Still, she thought only of protecting her mother. Maris had been ravaged by plague once in the past, and she was now a shadow of her former self, without the strength to stand against her attackers or endure their barrage.

"Stop it! Stop it! Stop iiiiit!"

The little girl's wails rang through the square, but the villagers' taunts beat her back down.

"Shut your trap, monster girl!"

"You dare use human words, you animal?"

"Why are you still alive?"

The words were like a stake being driven right into her heart. The girl felt a dark crack open up deep within her.

Why? It hurts... My heart... It hurts so bad...

As she cowered in fear, her eyes came to rest on her friends. Kril was swept up with the other villagers, shouting abuse and hurling stones, and there, by his side, pinching his sleeve in her hand and standing back where he couldn't see, was Lucia, her face pulled wide in a mocking smile.

Then the girl finally understood. In mind, body, and soul.

She betrayed me. She betrayed me. She betrayed me. She betrayed me!

"Why...? Why...?"

Tears trickled down the young girl's face. The stones bearing down drove the wedge deeper and deeper inside. Just as her heart was about to break completely, the rain of stones suddenly stopped.

"What's all this commotion?"

The men of the village had returned. They carried with them a humble number of wild beasts, the spoils of their hunting expedition.

"Father...! Father!"

Through teary eyes, the girl could just about make out the form of her father standing among them. He could make it stop. The villagers respected him, and everyone expected him to succeed the elder.

The villagers and her father conferred. She felt a wave of relief wash over her. Everything was going to be—

* * *

"No! I didn't know about any of this!"

"   "

The world began to turn. Her vision swirled before disappearing entirely.

"That woman tricked me, too! Those stinking creatures lied to me!"

She heard nothing, saw nothing, smelled nothing, felt nothing.

"What…is happening? Huh? I mean, what…?"

The last thing she heard was the sound of something shattering into a million pieces.

And then her world was annihilated.

The next thing she knew, she was being transported in a slave seller's cart. All she remembered was being sold off for next to nothing by the man she had once thought of as her father.

Her body declined to the point where she was practically paralyzed, but the girl still found the strength to go on because her mother was with her. She faced harsh treatment at the hands of her masters, even worse than the way the other slaves were being handled, and being an expensive commodity didn't lessen the disdain that beast-folk invited. She was given the worst food and beaten and whipped for no reason. If she was lucky, she got to bathe in the dirty water left over by everyone else, but otherwise, she didn't even get that, and her masters kicked her into the mud, sneering at her for being smelly and dirty. They even put a harness on her and made her pull the cart from time to time, calling it an animal's job.

Still, the girl persevered. She held on tight to what remained of her mind for the sake of her ailing mother. Yet for all she did to ease her mother's stress, it was no use. Her once sweet, loving mother became less and less. The slave owners were using her as a scapegoat. Seeing the awful things that were done to the beastfolk made the other slaves feel better about their own situations. *Look*, the other slaves seemed to be saying to each other. *At least you're not as bad off as them.*

And it worked. The others laughed at the beastfolk's treatment. When the girl was whipped and beaten, when her mother was dragged around by the hair, when they were both kicked to the ground, the slaves roared and howled like they were watching a comedy.

Six months after being sold into slavery, only half the distance to the royal capital, her mother's body gave up completely, and the girl's world shattered for the second time.

"*Tsk*. Broken, are you? You beastfolk ain't half as tough as I heard you were. Can't believe there are nobles into this crap. What's the world comin' to, I tell ya?"

The girl simply stared at the slave seller with vacant eyes.

"And yer mother's gone and snuffed it, too. Can't believe I'm out here lettin' you impact my bottom line."

With a twitch, something inside the girl reacted to his words.

Why...?

Something oozing like venom.

Why...? What did I do wrong? When did I become the enemy? What should I have done?

92

Something that burst up out of somewhere deep inside her and enveloped the remains of the girl's dark, lifeless heart.

Whose fault is it? Why am I here? Who am I? Why do I exist? What do I feel?

The thoughts pressed down on the remains of her heart, heating them like magma deep underground. Wriggling, coiling, churning, those fragments were warped beyond all recognition.

When her heart was reforged, it held only a single, pure emotion.

"Oh. I want to destroy."

That realization was a single droplet that heralded the storm of emotion she had been holding back.

...I despise them.

I am consumed by hate, hate, hate, hate, hate, hate, hate, hate, hate. Raw hate.

I hate Lucia. I hate Kril. I hate the man who was once my father. I hate the elder and all the villagers.

I hate the slavers who made me and my mother into laughingstocks, and I hate the slaves who laughed at us.

I want to hurt them and wound them and bend them and break them and grind them and slash them and cut them and blind them and slice them and choke them and burn them and split them and stab them and skin them and tear them and squash them. I want to kill them. I want to kill them. Kill them. Kill them. Kill them. Kill them. Kill them. Kill them. KILL THEM!

*   *   *

The thoughts covered her mind until there was nothing else left.

After that, she didn't listen to anything the slaver sellers told her anymore. Whenever she disobeyed, she was beaten, whipped, starved, or whatever else they could think of, but nothing extinguished the fire within her. When she was so broken that she couldn't move, when she was close to death, her flame yet burned. When sellers at the capital imprinted her with her Slave Brand and used it to inflict extreme pain, she glared back at her captors with unbridled malice. Before long, they gave up on feeding her, changing her, and bathing her and left her to rot in her cage. She spent her days imagining her brutal revenge and how she would tear her enemies limb from limb. Soon enough, even those days would end. She was going to die.

Despite being faced with this knowledge, the fire worming around inside her would not stop.

But even the hardiest beastfolk did not last long without food. Her mind was already fading, and all she could feel anymore was the burning heat at her core.

"Ah, what brilliant eyes."

A voice cut through her haze. A stranger was looking at her. These nobles from the capital were all the same. Many had visited, but this time, she had not the strength to lash out like before. The only thing she could do was glare with all the hate in her heart.

But when she looked into that boy's eyes, she felt something deeply familiar.

"Don't...touch...me...human."

Already, her parched, cracked lips had spoken.

"Grh! Aaaaaaaarghhh!"

Then a flashing pain ran through her body and penetrated her clouded mind. It felt like her scars were going to burst, and a piercing scream escaped her. Just as the waves of pain subsided, the boy poured a strange liquid down her throat.

"Nglg! Glglg! Gluuughhh!"

She hadn't even the strength to spit it back up. However, seconds after she ingested the mysterious fluid, her tired bones felt the faint spark of life. Having not had decent food or rest for days had rendered her body barren of mana, but now it felt at about half charged.

"Now maybe you're feeling well enough to talk to me."

The girl could not comprehend what the man standing before her was saying. Her recovering mind was only barely able to understand that she had just drunk some HP and MP potions. They weren't something you'd give to a slave. They might not be entirely out of reach for the public, but they were still expensive.

"What...?" she began.

The girl had plenty of cause to suspect some kind of trap or other ruse, so the boy's next words came as quite a surprise.

"Who is it you want to kill?"

It was the greatest shock she'd felt since her mother's passing, when the slaver had said the words that caused her mind to break.

"Who do you want revenge on?"

Looking closer, she saw that the boy's eyes didn't seem too different from her own. She realized why they felt so familiar. They held the same heat that dwelled within her. His eyes were her eyes. Her answer to his question was immediate.

"My best friends. My father. The village elder and all the villagers. The slavers and the other slaves."

"Is killing them all you want to do?"

He asked it like he already knew the answer. Of course he did, but he wanted her to say it. And she would. She would say it as many times as it needed to be said, until she no longer had to think about it. Until it became instinct, etched onto her heart.

"No. Death is too good for them. I want to make them suffer, hurt, weep, and wail. Then I want to break them. Slowly. They have to be fully broken when they die; otherwise, it's just a waste."

She smiled her first smile since becoming a slave. The boy before her, too, smiled at her words.

"Death is too good for them. I want to make them suffer, hurt, weep, and wail. Then I want to break them. Slowly. They have to be fully broken when they die; otherwise, it's just a waste."

The words of the broken girl brought a smile to my face.

"I have laid out two paths for you," I told her. "On the first, we are master and servant, nothing more. When I have fulfilled your use, I will grant you money and power enough to survive on your own. I will release you from your slavery. You could live a long, happy, and fulfilling life."

"..."

"You could rid yourself of the darkness inside your heart. Hide the scratches on your soul and pretend that none of it ever happened. A happy future full of laughter, one where you can smile."

It was a joke on my part. Both she and I knew that our minds were made up. Still, I had to put it into words, if only to remind her of what might have been. We didn't know what the future held. Perhaps one day, we would come to regret our choice. That was why I had to offer her another possibility, one that we could not turn back from.

"The second path for us to become comp...no, al..."

I stopped midsentence.

"Hmm... Neither of those words sound right," I muttered to myself. *Companion? Ally?* That wasn't what I came here for. Our relationship couldn't be summed up with empty platitudes. Our bond was nothing so weak. There was only one thing to call a pact such as ours. A name for those spurned by the world, who spurned it in turn. A name for those who chose death over life, sin over virtue, retribution over redemption.

"The second path is to become my partner in crime. To embrace revenge, and to revel in its execution."

I extended my hand, and a soul blade formed in the air above it. Black wisps coalesced into the form of a short sword with a double-edged blade that was shaped like a flame. Twisted up its fifty-centimeter length were red markings, the color of blood. Staring at it was like peering into the endless void. To gaze upon it was to bear witness to one's own divine judgment. If I wanted, I could will it into the shape of a longsword for use in battle, but right now, this form was ideal.

Grasping the hilt of the Holy Sword of Retribution, I sliced the girl's fetters clean off her body before embedding the blade in the ground before her.

"If you pick the former, then turn around. If the latter, then take the blade. Don't make this decision lightly. There's no going back. Once you grab hold of this sword, you will be irreparably damaged— tainted, cursed never again to lead a normal life. Cursed never to find rest until vengeance is yours."

"…"

"That sword will transform the heat burning inside you into a raging flame that will never go out. Try as you might, you will never be able to give up on your revenge. When you take this blade, your enemies will become my enemies, and mine yours. The hate I feel will become your hate, and your hate will become mine. Oh, and supposedly, you should get a new intrinsic skill based on your talents."

"…Are you going to betray me?"

The girl's eyes seemed to go on forever, a darkness without end. Oh, I knew. I knew my word wouldn't cut it here.

"Once you accept this pact, we will no longer be able to harm each other. If one of us dies, so will the other," I explained.

There was a flicker of understanding in the girl's eyes. Not only did this contract prevent me from betraying her, but it also prevented her from betraying me. I didn't want to be backstabbed again, after all, nor did I want to backstab anyone and end up just like those I hated the most. If it wasn't for the power to enforce this contract, I wouldn't be here offering this deal in the first place.

Having said all I needed to say, I released the hilt of the blade.

"Of course, you could always seek revenge on your own. My enemies are many, and you might not want to take on that much hate. Still, it would make me extremely happy if you accepted."

"…Why?" the girl asked, but I knew she harbored no suspicion. She already knew what I would say. She was simply confirming that we were one and the same.

A maniacal grin spread across my face.

"Isn't it obvious? Two is more fun than one. Two can come up with much better plans, put much more effort into torturing our targets, breaking them, grinding them down into mush. People who just want to kill are of *no use* to me, but you aren't like that, are you?"

"Ah! Ah-ha-ha-ha!" The girl, overjoyed at my words, broke into laughter. "I like the sound of that. 'Partners in crime,' you say? You have a point. If I'm with you, my revenge could be all the sweeter. Together, we could drive them into far greater depths of despair than I ever could alone." The girl's gentle smile was worthy of the Virgin Mary, but her eyes shone with a mad glint. "In that case, there's nothing left to think about. My flame of revenge will never die? Good. I don't want to go back to those simple days spent stoking a smoldering heart. Taking on extra enemies is nothing compared with the thought of returning to that disgusting life I used to lead. The fact that it helps my revenge is just icing on the cake."

"Then take the sword. It will show you what to do."

Sure enough, she gripped the Holy Sword of Retribution by the hilt and removed it from the ground. As she did, the blade emitted a blinding black light that scorched the eyes. That was proof that it recognized her lust for revenge. That paradoxical light was a blessing upon her journey.

"Ah," I said, "come to think of it, I haven't asked your name."

"My name? My name is Minnalis."

"I see. I am Kaito Ukei."

"Kaito Ukei... My master's name is Kaito Ukei."

For the first time, Minnalis smiled a peaceful smile. Then she leveled the point of the sword to her heart.

"It's a pleasure to be working with you, Minnalis."

"Likewise, Master," she replied, then plunged the blade deep into her own chest.

The blade emitted a burning light before rapidly dissipating into shimmering motes. There was no wound on Minnalis's body, nor so much as a hole in her dirty rags.

"I see," I mused. "So this is the reason behind your revenge."

"I just saw the motive behind your actions."

The Holy Sword of Retribution had woven our two paths together, combining our vengeance into one.

It had forced us each to experience firsthand the origins of the other's hate. I felt the pain and despair that she felt when she swore her oath, as though it were me in her shoes. It burned me up from the inside, a black heat no less equal to the one I already bore. Minnalis, too, winced in pain as she saw why I walked the path of revenge.

As our bitter hearts, two black lumps of charred coal, grew closer, they merged into something purer, something we shared as one. By the time the motes of black light that were left behind by the Holy Sword of Retribution disappeared completely, there was no longer any meaningful difference between the two of us.

"It feels like I was the one your village betrayed, even though I know in my mind that wasn't the case," I observed. "So this is what it means to share revenge."

I looked around at the faces of the other slaves, who'd mocked her, who'd cheered at her abuse, and my blood boiled. The slaves, sensing danger, shrunk into the corners of their cages, terrified, and looked at me with hollow, lifeless eyes.

System message: Title acquired: "Avenger's Master."

System message: Individual Minnalis has become "Slave to Revenge."

The system message informed me that the sword's effect had worked as intended. I looked at Minnalis. She seemed a little bewildered, and a little excited.

"Wow," she breathed out. "Is this all because of that sword? Ohhh… Ohhhh, this is going to be even better than I imagined!"

The thought of it gave her the shivers, and her face froze in a look of ecstatic pleasure.

"Open Status: Minnalis," I declared. Her status screen appeared, and I could see the contents. The title "Avenger's Master" gave me access to the status screens of anyone with the title "Slave to Revenge." There were also other perks, such as stat buffs and bonus effects, based on the number of such servants I acquired. These titles were also the reason that our lust for revenge would not disappear and that we were shown each other's memories.

Looking at her screen, I could see that beastfolk stats were indeed high. Even though her stats were being halved by her Weak condition, she was still on par with a human of the same level.

She had also gained a new intrinsic ability. I was missing my appraisal soul blade, so I couldn't tell what it did, but the possessor of an ability knew its effects, so I could always just ask her to explain it.

"So? What now? You know, if you're tired, you can take a break. Leave all the hard work to me."

"Well now, my new master appears to be quite the tease. You wouldn't deny me my first act of vengeance, would you?"

"Of course not. In that case, I'll leave things here in your capable hands and go bring you the *other one* who got away."

I handed my remaining MP potions to Minnalis. I didn't know what she was going to do, but given what we had talked about, I imagined that it involved her intrinsic ability. That would require a lot of MP, and I wanted to give her the best shot at revenge I could.

Then I left, in pursuit of the man who had fled.

STATUS

Minnalis   Lv18

Age 16 • Female • Lagonid

HP: 160/208 (416)   MP: 189/206 (412)

Strength: 105 (211)   Stamina: 111 (222)

Vitality: 85 (171)   Dexterity: 139 (278)

Magic: 123 (247)   Resistance: 95 (191)

Intrinsic Abilities: Intoxicating Phantasm

Skills: Illusion Magic Lv 3, Pain Resistance Lv 2,

Harvest Lv 2

Status: Weak

The slave seller made his escape around the time the strange man dressed in black conjured an ominous-looking short sword out of nowhere.

He found the man suspicious at first, but all that mattered to him was whether he could pay. When the man said he would pay up to ten gold coins for slaves with a market price of four at best, he knew he had a chump on his hands. He could sell him some expensive slaves at a significant markup and rake in the cash.

But then the man asked about that Lagonid girl. A worthless beast who was left in her cage to die because it cost too much to even *feed* her. Surely, even this naive man wouldn't pay much for her, and so the slave seller was just about to steer him toward some pricier slaves when the man declared he would pay ten gold coins for her.

What luck! Ten gold coins for a product he was just going to throw away. The slave seller thought it must have been his lucky day, and he rubbed his hands, imagining all that free profit.

Things took a strange turn not long after the contract was signed, when the man gave his new slave some expensive potions to drink. Then they talked for a bit. The slave seller couldn't quite follow, but their conversation was disturbing all the same. The breaking point was when the customer pulled out a black-and-red blade—a terrifying weapon. He didn't need to know what it was to see that it was a bad sign.

The slaver knew danger. He did business in the slums, after all, and his survival instincts were telling him to get out of there as quickly as possible. His slaves and his money wouldn't matter if he wasn't alive to enjoy them. He slipped away while the two were talking and flew out into the street, taking only a bag of gold that he kept behind the counter for emergencies.

He didn't look back; he just ran in search of the safe house he had prepared for such an eventuality. Tripping over himself and losing his way several times, he eventually arrived at its door.

"Hey, now. You wouldn't leave a customer waiting, would you?"

The man stood before his very eyes, wearing a smile in name only.

"Ah! Er…um…well, you see, I had an emergency to attend to…," the slave seller stammered, his face pale, before making a break for one of the side alleys nearby.

I wasn't about to let him escape, for he was now one of my sworn enemies. I knocked him out with a blow to the back of the head. I had to be careful; too much force could break his neck, and we didn't want him to die just yet. It would be awfully rude of me to start the *meal* without my partner, after all. I planned to take a purely advisory role this time, but I figured I may as well be proactive and find out some information about the slave seller that Minnalis would find useful.

The Holy Sword of Retribution only showed me the moment her desire for revenge took root, so I knew nothing about Minnalis's enemies except for this man. I needed to talk about all of them and learn how to make them all suffer. If all I had was my own hate, I couldn't do anything except kill them immediately.

I lifted the unconscious man onto my shoulder and made my way back to the slave market. When I returned, Minnalis had herded all the slaves into the largest cage, and she was working on something in the cooking area at the back of the shop. There was still a little room in the cage, despite there being about twenty slaves crammed in there.

"Hey. Got him for you," I announced.

"Ah, thank you, Master. My hands are full right now, so please just throw him in there with the rest of them."

"Hmm? Okay."

"Gah…!"

I unlocked the cage, which was attached to the wall, and tossed the man inside before relocking it. As he hit the hard stone floor, he came to his senses and looked around in confusion.

"Y-you bastard! Do you have any idea what you're—?!"

"I'm dooone! Whoa… I'm so dizzy all of a sudden…" The man was interrupted by a jubilant cry that came from the kitchen and seemed totally inappropriate. Technically, this level of excitement was just right for what was about to happen.

Minnalis appeared, looking a little unsteady, with the most beautiful smile on her face.

"That's what happens when you use all your MP up at once. Hurry up and drink the potion I gave you."

"Yes, Master… Tee-hee… Hey, will you give it to me mouth-to-mouth…?"

"No."

"Awww, why nooot?"

"You're just high from the MP loss. I'm not so thirsty that I'd take advantage of a girl in that state."

MP loss led to a sensation of drunkenness. Using a decent amount in one go would just cause headaches and a sensation of *dizziness*, but go beyond that, and it could feel like you'd been out drinking all night, complete with a loss of inhibitions. Restoring your MP wouldn't instantly sober you up, either, so you had to be careful.

Checking her status, I saw that her MP had gone from the 90 percent she'd had when I left her, down to about 10 percent. It was quite a lot, considering that an average fireball you'd use in battle consumed only ten MP.

Minnalis was already excited enough from getting to use her new power and exact her vengeance. I was probably going to need to give her some space the next morning.

Meanwhile, Minnalis had taken the MP potion and was guzzling the blue liquid in a most provocative manner.

"*Phew...* Master, you are such a tease."

"Come on. Stop messing around. Isn't it about time to start on the main dish?"

"Yep! Hee-hee!"

It appeared Minnalis required no further assistance from me, so I sat back to enjoy the spectacle. With a buoyant mood that refused to acknowledge the bleak atmosphere of the room, she happily *carried the food she had prepared over to the cage*. It took several trips. She'd used up everything the slave seller kept in his stores.

"Here you go; food's ready! Eat up!"

The smell of the meal was divine, but as expected, neither the shopkeeper nor the slaves would even touch it. They just stared at Minnalis with apprehension.

"Hmm, I guess you guys don't want to eat my cooking... Then why don't we start with you? You were giving such a dirty, rotten look to me and my mother the entire way to the capital."

"Eek!"

Still smiling, Minnalis glared at one of the manacled slaves with the look of a predator eyeing up its prey. As her mana surged, the color disappeared from her beige eyes, replaced with a gray haze that glowed with a dim, faded light.

"Mind turn to chaos. *Intoxicating Phantasm.*"

Her words were gentle, beguiling, and emotionless, like a witch.

"Aaah! Aaaaahhh! What's happening?! Make it stopppp!"

Her mana merged into a pale mist that enveloped the man. The other slaves and the dealer could do nothing but watch, their faces pale with terror as they struggled to comprehend what was going on. The mist dissolved into the man as though it were being absorbed through his skin, and he wailed madly.

"Graaarh! Aaaargh! Give me the food! Give it to meeee!"

He launched himself toward the bars as though he had forgotten he was shackled, and when he tripped and fell to the ground, he still crawled desperately on all fours, like an animal. He grabbed fistfuls of the steaming-hot food and shoveled it into his mouth without a shred of dignity.

"Ohhh, this stuff is stronger than I thought. Look how hungry he thinks he is now! It's going to take some experimenting to get the level just right."

Minnalis cackled as she watched the ravenous man. The other prisoners were starting to feel uneasy. All she had done was make him eat some food. They were expecting something far crueler from her.

"Now," she said, "it's time for the rest of you to eat up. Don't worry, I'll be gentler this time and let you slowly give in to madness as your hunger grows... Mind, stir. *Intoxicating Phantasm*."

"Wha...? Urp..."

"Ah... Uhhh..."

"Wargh... Urgh..."

The pale mist appeared once again and coiled around the men before sinking into their bodies. This time, they didn't instantly make a mad dash for the food, but they still approached it timidly. Just a couple of them reached out at first, but with time, all of them gave in to the hunger, and before long, they were all feasting to their hearts' content.

Minnalis grinned and looked at them fondly, like she was watching a plant she helped grow. Soon, it would bear fruit. Very soon now.

"Urgh? Argh... GRAAAARGH!!"

"Ah, there it is! ♪"

The first to react was the man she had first used her magic on. Minnalis's expression transformed into a wicked grin.

"Gah! Urgh! Aaaaaaaargh!"

His arms were the first to change. His tanned, muscular arms became shriveled *and green, like a goblin's.* The other slaves froze mid-meal and stared at him in astonishment. The man writhed in pain and gazed blankly at his transformed arms. However, it was not for long; soon after he stopped eating, his ravenous hunger consumed him once more, and he rushed back toward the food.

"Now, eat up, my lovelies. The more you eat, the more you transform into a goblin! I hope that doesn't bother you. If so, no matter. Soon, your hunger will be so great, you won't be able to control yourself. Hee-hee-hee!"

"No! Noooooo!"

"Urgh! Gah! Urp!"

"Gaaaah! Ugh! Grrrrrrah!"

Most of the prisoners began vomiting up their undigested food, but their hunger kept growing, snowballing out of control as if mocking their attempts at fighting back.

"Aaagh! Gah! No! I can't eat! But I'm so HUNGRYYYYYYY!"

"*Huff, huff, huff, huff.* I don't care. I don't care anymooooreee!"

No matter how they tried to resist, all of them succumbed to their hunger and resumed eating. Then soon, they began to transform.

"Graaaaah!"

Minnalis watched them through the iron bars of the cage and stamped on a spindly green arm that reached out through them. Even after wincing in pain, the creature quickly got back to scooping up more food.

"Hee-hee-hee! You just can't keep your hands off my food, can you? Eat as much as you like! There's plenty more where that came from!"

"Gah... Gaaaaaargh!"

One particularly anguished scream rose out above the sounds of the feasting prisoners. However, this was not anguish at his transformation.

"Oh my, you've turned completely into a goblin now. I'm glad to see you love my food so much. Hee-hee!"

The man who first started eating was also the first to complete his transformation; he started scratching and clawing at his own body, his repulsive face stretched even uglier in pain. Yet even now, he didn't stop eating and continued to shove food into his mouth.

"One thing I should mention: This food is lethal to monsters; it causes them to die the most horrific, painful deaths. How does it feel to eat it knowing that? Are you listening to me? Well, I suppose you can't answer. After all, goblins can't say anything except *Gah*."

By this point, most of the prisoners had transformed into goblins and were clawing hysterically at the food. The more they ate, the closer to goblins they became, and the more the food racked their bodies with unbearable pain as it killed them. They could not stop eating, even though the last vestiges of their minds knew what it was doing to them. Their survival instincts knew only that they had to eat, and it overpowered what little reason they had left.

Minnalis gazed at the cage of goblins that used to be her owner and fellow slaves with a look of pure satisfaction, like her heart had been set free.

"Ah-ha-ha-ha-ha-ha! Die, die, die! Suffer and perish, powerless to do anything about it! Feel the helplessness I felt when my mom passed away and die as wretchedly as she did! Ah-ha-ha! Ah-ha-ha-ha-ha!"

One goblin stuck its head out through the bars toward the food, even as it suffered. It was impossible to tell who it had once been. Seeing this, Minnalis stamped on the goblin's head, pressing it down into the fatal meal.

"Ah-ha-ha-ha! Still hungry, are we? Ah-ha-ha! Ah-ha-ha-ha-ha-ha!"

Minnalis's wild laughter continued until the very last of the goblins' shrieks had ended.

It had not taken long for every living thing in that cage to cease breathing. A pile of goblin corpses marked the success of the first step in Minnalis's revenge. The heat that burned inside her was now my heat, too, and it exploded into rapturous delight within me. Watching them claw for that food, even knowing that it was going to kill them, was so much fun that I thought my sides were going to split. It sent shivers up my spine every time one of them screamed with the pain of transformation or retched as the poison killed them from within.

"Wonderful. Wonderful work, Minnalis. To make them feel hunger and then plant goblin-transformation and monster-killing poisons in their food. Heh, I knew I was right to pick you— Ah!"

I had accidentally said what I was thinking out loud. I was just so happy. She had thought long and hard about how best to make them suffer. She had shown to me beautiful proof that her words had been sincere all along. I was giddy with excitement at watching her take the first step down her path of revenge.

"Ahhh, I did it. I finally did it. The first part's over, Mom."

Minnalis opened the cage and approached the pile of bodies, her hands clasped in prayer. Her face was peaceful, and her gait solemn as she basked in the aftertaste of the forbidden fruit her patience had borne. She was a true avenger, and I simply watched her in silence, without interrupting her trance.

*   *   *

That day, a slave market in the slums closed down, and the slaves disappeared. The building went untouched until a few days later, when a robber broke in.

All the robber found there was an indescribable stench and a cage full of rotting goblin corpses.

"Well, I suppose we'd better be on our way."

As much as I would have loved to stay there, appreciating the beauty of the moment forever, we had to be moving on, and I clapped Minnalis on the shoulder.

"...Yes. I must thank you, Master. It was your power that allowed me to exact such delicious revenge."

"No need to thank me. My power is your power, and your desires are my desires. The moment you chose to seek vengeance, our paths became intertwined. This is no mere transactional relationship we share. We're partners in crime, remember?"

Minnalis shook her head.

"It may have been my choice, but it was you who gave me that decision. I chose you, Master. That is why you are the one who is owed thanks for this vengeance I now bear. You gave me the opportunity to take my revenge, when I could only sit powerlessly as the heat smoldered inside me and I waited for death. The only thing I truly consider mine is this anger, and even that I now share with you. I offer everything else I am to you in its entirety. You can have my body, my soul, my life, to do with as you please."

"I don't need any of that. Calm down."

"Oh, Master! ♪ You're such a tease...! ♪"

Minnalis wrapped her body around me. I pushed her away. The

girl was a full head shorter than me, and despite her shabby appearance, there was a strange lust in her flushed cheeks and tear-stained eyes. She chuckled, and it sent a shiver down my spine. It felt like she was a predator eyeing up her next meal.

The MP drunkenness must still be affecting her. Depleting and restoring her MP so much was causing her conscious mind to recede, and her animal instincts were coming to the fore.

I just need to bear with it. She'll calm down eventually, and when she does, her sexual urges should disappear, too.

If you just ignored drunks, they stopped being a problem. It was only because you gave them attention that they kept bothering you.

"Let's get going; we've only just started down the path of revenge. There's still much further to go. Save your thanks for when it's done. Or are you telling me this was enough to sate the vengeance within you?"

"No, you're right, Master. I must keep improving, so that the fruits we taste are sweeter than ever before! Hee-hee! Ah, my mind swims at the possibilities!"

…This…is going to wear off…right? I can't have her acting like this the whole time…

I left the building. Some time had passed, and it was now afternoon. Clocks were something of a luxury in this world, and so the only ways to tell the time were to go by the position of the sun or the chiming of the church bell.

I glanced at Minnalis, who was walking alongside me, and decided it would be best to head into the city and buy her some decent clothes.

"Ah, could you hide your ears and tail? If not, we'll buy something here in the slums to cover them up before heading into town."

"Don't worry, Master. I still have a lot of MP left, so I'll just use my illusion magic."

Minnalis wove her mana skillfully, and her rabbit features

disappeared in a puff of smoke. Even with her "Illusion Magic" skill at level 3, perfectly executing a spell like that while skipping the verbal components was no mean feat.

"..."

"Eek! M-Master?"

Examining the spot where her ears had been, I found that my hand encountered the softest and fluffiest sensation.

"Mmm... Ah... Master... Not there..."

"Ah, sorry, I was just curious."

Minnalis's sensual voice brought me back to my senses, and I withdrew my hand. The first time around, I'd only been interested in slaying the demon lord and getting back to my own world as soon as possible, so I ended up ignoring many of this world's mythical features. While I was never sitting idle, I still felt like I had wasted my time somehow.

"I suppose we should talk about what we want to do next. Personally, I was planning on leaving town sometime today."

"*Phew...*" Minnalis paused to catch her breath. "Today?" she asked, looking dubiously up at the sky.

I understood what she was getting at. The sun would only be up for another hour or so, and the four gates in each direction, which permitted entry to the city, were closed at night, making it practically impossible to leave. Even if we made it in time, the closest neighboring towns were half a day's travel away. That was why when people had to go somewhere, they usually set off in the morning.

"You saw for yourself how many enemies I have. The king, queen, princess, and all the royal knights. Well, I gave the princess and the knights a little preview yesterday. I'd guess around this time tomorrow, they'll be able to talk again, and I'd like to be out of the city before then. I'm not strong enough to stand against them yet, so we don't have much time. Come to think of it, what's the last memory of mine that you can vicariously see?"

The Holy Sword of Retribution didn't reveal everything. I doubted that it showed her my memories from the start of my second chance, since those were all after I swore revenge. But that would mean...

"Hmm? Now that you mention it, it didn't make much sense. Are you a ghost, Master? What was all that about you being a hero and the world turning against you...?"

"Thought so. You saw up to my death. I also only saw the crucial moments of your life. I'll explain everything later, so just bear with me for now."

Minnalis nodded, though she still looked confused. "Okay, Master. In that case, let's get the bare minimum food and clothing and leave this place as soon as we can."

"Hmm? Oh, no, we don't need to go that fast. I plan to *leave at night.* Hold on, aren't you a little put off by the fact that the whole royal family is my enemy?"

We were talking about antagonizing the royalty in a land where the crown wielded absolute power. It was the same as the country itself being after you.

"Well, sure, I was a little surprised, but the important thing is that they're your enemies. We've agreed to take revenge on them no matter the cost, right? The fact that they're royalty doesn't change any of that." She smiled, almost as though the thought of it excited her.

"...Heh, you win," I said, raising my hands in surrender. "It was a dumb question, I suppose. I really am glad to have you as my partner in crime."

I had been underestimating her. Even if she stayed in that weird mood forever, she'd still be the best partner I could ever ask for.

"Oh! Well, yes. I suppose I'm also quite happy I joined forces with you, Master."

For a moment, she almost looked embarrassed, but she quickly recovered and gave a slight smile. It seemed she was still a little tipsy.

"First, we'd better do something about your clothes. We'll need traveling clothes that hide your ears and tail, and a weapon for you to defend yourself. Also, food."

"Hold on, Master. How are you planning to leave the city at night? The gates will close soon."

"Hmm? Oh, don't worry, we won't be using the gates. *We'll be leaving through a hole in the walls.*"

"Th-there's a hole in the walls?" Minnalis asked, bewildered.

The walls were the city's last defense against a monster attack. Any damage to them would constitute a grave threat to national security. That was why the wall had Self-Repair and Degradation Down enchantments. It was hard to imagine what kind of force would be necessary to blow a hole in it that was large enough for a person to go through. Under normal conditions, that is.

"There will be. Right now, the slightest damage will break it wide open. I know this for a fact," I revealed, giving her a smile.

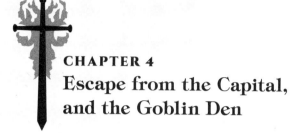

CHAPTER 4
Escape from the Capital, and the Goblin Den

A re you really okay with giving me such nice clothes?"
Minnalis had changed out of her slave attire, which was little more than tattered rags with holes torn in them for her arms and head, and into a set of clothing I had picked up at a secondhand store. The sky above was growing dim and bathed the streets of the city in a twilight glow. Despite her reaction, the clothes weren't that special—just a little above average of what the townsfolk might normally wear. If she was comparing them with what she had as a slave, then yes, they must have appeared quite nice indeed, but they were nothing to get excited about. While I was at it, I had also purchased an outfit for myself that allowed me to blend in more.

"It's fine. You're a beautiful woman, Minnalis. I'd rather you didn't look like a slave, or else the pigs and the monkeys wouldn't leave us alone," I said as I remembered a rather unpleasant memory with the nobility and the delinquents.

Slaves were treated as property, and if you walked down the street flaunting your expensive property, you'd run into two types of people. The pigs, who wanted to purchase it for themselves to show off their money and status, and the monkeys, who simply cornered you in a dark alley and shook you down for all you were worth.

I had to deal with that kind of greed the first time around, too. There was one particular noble who stuck out. He wasn't very good at concealing his desires, but he knew how to cover his ass so he would never get in trouble.

That said, delinquents were rare outside the slums, and the example I'd made was also very effective at keeping them at bay. The nobles, however, could still be a problem. I wanted us to stand out as little as possible right now. Getting into a commotion with an aristocrat was the last thing we needed.

The potions had removed all traces of the bruises across her body, and the dark circles around her eyes had disappeared, too. She was still looking a tad underfed, but anyone could tell she was gorgeous. If nobody suspected she was really a beastfolk, then as long as she looked like a slave, nobles would come out of the woodwork like termites, looking to buy her off me.

"...Beautiful? You...you think I'm beautiful? ... Hee-hee-hee!"

Minnalis stopped and shook, her face flushed. I turned and called to her.

"What's wrong? Does it still hurt? I guess the potions wouldn't have healed everything, huh?"

Restoring HP with potions recovered your physical energy, while replenishing your MP restored your mental strength. Both potions also restored Stamina, but it wasn't magic or poison that had caused Minnalis's Weak status; it was continuous exposure to a harsh environment. Even a status-healing potion wouldn't work on it. The only way to recover was with proper rest and good, nutritious food. For a beastfolk like her, that shouldn't take much longer than three days or so.

"I'm sorry, but we need to keep going to the item shop. We might not be able to cure your Weakness, but we might find something to make it a bit more bearable, and once we get out of the city, we can take things easy."

Potions came with a wide variety of effects. There were HP and MP recovery potions, of course, but there were also potions that gave temporary stat boosts, penalties, negated status conditions for a limited time, or even heightened your senses, allowing better use of skills.

Potions that dealt with status conditions came in two types: "recovery" potions, which dealt with the root cause, and "relief" potions, which only tackled the surface-level symptoms or merely weakened the condition's effect. One of those relief potions could be very useful for Minnalis right now. It wouldn't be a permanent solution, but it would make things a lot easier for her. Or so I thought, but Minnalis simply shook her head as if to say she was okay.

"Oh, it's fine; there's no need to go that far. My body just feels a little heavy, that's all. Besides, it seems that those goblins were counted as *defeated*, so I went up another level. I should be all right in another day or so."

Minnalis offered me a gentle smile, but her face still looked a little red to me. There was something wrong with her for sure, but she didn't seem willing to take a potion. If things got worse, I might have to force-feed her again, I thought, and I tried to walk slowly so she didn't fall behind.

I kept an eye on Minnalis as we walked, and sure enough, her condition didn't seem to be that big a deal. Whenever she looked at me, she flashed such a perfect smile that I couldn't imagine there was anything troubling her at all. Her face was no longer red, but she still appeared unusually reserved.

As we entered the item shop, I considered stocking up on relief potions anyway, just in case we needed them. It wasn't like we'd be out of the woods immediately after leaving the city. I bought some simple HP and MP potions, several status-recovery and status-relief potions, as well as a few days' worth of food and a good amount of seasoning.

"Here you go. I got you a Weakness relief potion. Drink up."

"N-no, I told you, I'm fine. I couldn't possibly take something so expensive."

"...Just shut up and drink it. I don't want to have to hold on to it."

Minnalis was reluctant, as I had predicted, so I gave her an order as her master. I wasn't about to use the Slave Brand on the exhausted girl, nor for that matter would I do it even if she were healthy. I would never resort to force to get her to do what I wanted. Having said that, her reluctance was going to cause us problems down the line, so I put my foot down, gave her a serious look, and lowered my voice to tell her it was important. It might have looked a little intimidating, but Minnalis was my partner in crime. We shared the same vengeance now, and she knew I wished her no harm. Hopefully, I wouldn't scare her. I was just trying to get across the gravity of the situation.

"I...I'm sorry, Master. I'll drink it."

I didn't mean for it to be such a big deal, but at last, Minnalis politely took the potion and downed it. I checked her status and saw that her condition had changed to *Weak (Poor)*, and her stats were reduced by a third instead of a half. Her face was looking red again, but I figured it would be okay once we got on the road.

The next stop on our list was the weapons and armor shop. I could fight with my soul blades, but Minnalis was going to need a weapon, and the two of us needed armor. Because her mana dropped off with distance, it made sense to gear her up as a close-range fighter, but she shouldn't have to fight barehanded. It wouldn't be the worst idea in the world with her stats, but her Intoxicating Phantasm ability was based on poison, as the name implied. It would be more effective if she could inflict slashing damage with a knife or sword, rather than the blunt damage of unarmed strikes.

"Minnalis, do you know much about weapons?" I asked.

Judging by her skills, she had no firsthand experience, but even if she was just a little familiar with a particular type, it would make things easier. I suppose she could also use her bare hands, or rather, her claws. There were many kinds of fighting styles, so to begin with, I wanted to pick a weapon that was easy for her to use.

"No... Sometimes, the adventurers who guarded the merchant caravans that came to our village would teach me how to swing a sword, but that's about it... I'm sorry."

"Hmm? You don't need to apologize. There's time for you to learn, and it's not your skill in combat that I chose you for. I bought you because you had what it took to be my partner in crime."

At that point, we arrived in front of the weapons and armor shop. It was a warm and unconventional (read: shabby) storefront near the border to the slums, with a carved wooden sign hanging outside that read LIECIAL WEAPONS AND ARMOR.

"Hey, welcome!" A young boy, the apprentice, greeted us as we walked in. "I'm sorry, but we're about to close for the day. I'd hate to rush you, so maybe you could come back tomorrow...?"

It was certainly getting late enough to be called dusk. Taverns were lighting their lamps and serving up ale for the evening.

"It's okay; I already know what I'm going to buy. It doesn't have to be anything special, so it shouldn't take long, and it's kind of urgent that I get it done today."

"I suppose that should be all right... Boss! There's a customer here!"

While Minnalis was gazing, starry-eyed, at all the new and exciting merchandise, a loud voice came back from the rear of the shop, where the boss appeared to be working on something.

"Huh? Tell 'em to get lost! When are we meant to eat if we've got people oohing and ahhing over weapons an' armor all night?!"

"He says he already knows what he wants!"

"Then sell 'im it, you numpty, and get 'im outta here!"

The apprentice turned back to me. "Okay, what would you like?"

"Two sets of novice adventurer gear, four sets of repair tools, and ten mass-produced longswords with scabbards. Whichever ones you choose are fine."

"That's a lot! Excuse me, sir, but can you pay for all that?"

The boy eyed me suspiciously. Not surprising, since what I had just asked for totaled about a month's wages (roughly twenty large-silver pieces), and I looked no richer than a normal citizen. I felt Minnalis beside me getting annoyed, so I hurried to smooth things over.

"Yes, I can. Here," I said, producing a single gold piece from my pouch. The boy's eyes went wide, and he apologized.

"Is that…a gold coin? Sorry, er, I mean, pardon me, sir! I've been so rude!"

"Oh, don't worry. I'm not acting on behalf of a noble or anything. It's just that I've come into a bit of money recently, you see."

The fact that I wasn't a noble myself was probably clear from the way I was dressed, but that gold coin had still given him the wrong idea. It wasn't strange for one acting on behalf of a powerful individual to abuse that power, and nobody wanted to be on the receiving end of a nobleman's wrath, so it was best to avoid offending such people wherever possible.

"Re-really?"

"It's true. Cross my heart."

My playful response seemed to calm his nerves somewhat, and he gave a short sigh as though deflating.

"I'm really sorry for doubting you, sir. I'll go get them now.

Two novice adventurer's armor sets, four repair kits, and ten mass-produced longswords, was it?"

"That's it, thanks."

The young man ran about the store, gathering up the items I had requested and placing them atop the counter.

"Here you are, two novice adventurer's armor sets, four repair kits, and ten mass-produced longswords. That's five silvers times two, which is one large silver, plus two large coppers times four, seven…no, eight, plus one silver and five large coppers times ten, which is…er… one large silver and five silvers. So in total, that makes…um… Ow!"

A beefy fist came down on the young man's head as he desperately tried to count on his fingers.

"How long are you gonna stand there dawdling? You should be able to do sums in yer 'ead!"

A rather impressively built older craftsman lumbered out of the back of the shop.

"That's nothing to hit me for!" the apprentice squealed. "It's not gonna make me go any faster!"

"Don't you talk back to me, you little runt!"

"Ow, ow, ow, ow!"

The man's face was stern, and his beard thick. It was a testament to his dwarf blood. One-quarter, if I remembered correctly.

"Master? Is something the matter?" asked Minnalis. It seemed she had noticed the bittersweet expression on my face.

That was because these two were killed the first time around, and it was all my fault. I had told the princess about their heritage, oblivious to her complete disdain for foreigners, and she put both father and son to death. Apart from their beards and small stature, dwarves were very similar to humans in every way. For a man who was only one-quarter dwarf, and especially his son, who was only one-eighth, it was hard to distinguish them from humans. I had been led to believe they went back to their hometown, and I only learned the truth when the princess herself admitted it to me.

I'd listened in despair as she thanked me for helping rid her country of vermin.

I knew it had been foolish of me to come here, but I had to see them again, even if just for sentimental reasons. Maybe if they had survived, they would have simply turned against me like everyone else. I didn't know. They'd never lived that long. But at the very least, while I knew them, they'd never once betrayed me. And so while I hated the people of this country with a burning passion, all I felt when I looked at these two was guilt.

I never meant to let my emotions show through so plainly. Was Minnalis always so perceptive, or was it because of the new bond we shared? I didn't know the answer to that.

"It's nothing." I shook my head. I didn't have the time to explain it to her now.

"The stuff on the table," started the shopkeeper, "comes to two large silvers, five silvers, and eight large coppers. You can adjust the size of the leather armor by fiddlin' with the straps, but if it still don't fit, we can fix it for you for one silver apiece. As for the swords, I don't know what you want ten of 'em for, but if they get scuffed up so bad that you can't mend 'em with those repair kits, we can reforge 'em for you for about a silver each, too. That depends on how damaged they are, of course. Anything else you want to know?"

"Is it all right if we change into our armor here? We've got a lot to carry."

I placed a gold coin onto the counter and received my change in large and regular silvers.

"Go ahead. You need me to show you how to put it on?"

"I know how to do it, and I'll help her myself. It's not too hard."

The armor set comprised a leather breastplate and waist guard, along with leggings and gauntlets, which were both made of leather and iron. I quickly put my own set on, then gave Minnalis a hand with hers. The reason I refused the shopkeeper's help was because although Minnalis's ears and tail were invisible, they were technically still there, and the shopkeeper might stumble upon her true identity if we weren't careful. I wanted to believe that these two wouldn't sell us out, but I knew how people who were close to me could switch sides when their circumstances changed. I knew it all too well.

"Mph... Kaito...you're hurting my chest..."

"Oh, sorry. I pulled too tightly."

I was lost in thought and had used more force than necessary. The tightness was squeezing her sizable breasts, causing them to spill over. As I hurried to loosen the straps, the shopkeeper clapped me on the shoulder and gave me a thumbs-up.

"Nice work, lad!"

"Shut up, old man! Have some self-respect in front of your son!"

"Huh?" asked the son. "What's that about me? Is something happening I should know about?"

The shopkeeper was as shameless as ever. It was partly why we got on so well last time, but it was also a pity, as it was the only blemish upon his otherwise outstanding character. I loosened Minnalis's armor and attached two of the swords to her belt, while I bundled the others together using the cord on their scabbards and carried them myself.

"Sorry for stopping by when you were about to close. Oh, I know, I'll tell you something I heard to make up for it. Apparently, antidotes are about to jump in price. I'd stock up on them while you can."

"Huh. That right? I'll keep that in mind," replied the shopkeeper.

"Heh, yes, that should do it... And I'm sorry for last time."

"Hmm? What's that?"

"Nothing. Just some closure. Well, see you."

I left the shopkeeper, who was looking somewhat puzzled, and exited the shop with Minnalis. Outside, the sun had pretty much set.

"Let me carry that," she offered, pointing at my purchases. "I'm your slave, after all."

"I don't want anyone to know that, remember."

"Well, even if I weren't your slave, I still think I should help out..."

"It'll look weird if a girl is lugging all my heavy things and I'm empty-handed. Besides, you're already carrying our food. This is fine as it is."

Minnalis still looked concerned, but I ignored her. It was certainly convenient that she made efforts to be proactive and respect our master-slave relationship, but I didn't want her to be stuck always thinking she was below me. Minnalis wasn't just my slave; she was my partner in crime. After seeing how well she performed, it would be a waste of her talents if she just did whatever I told her when it came time to plan our revenge. I would have to keep a close eye on how she viewed our relationship from here on out.

"Anyway, that should be all we need. Let's be aware of our surroundings and get out of here."

The sun had disappeared completely, and the moon shone in the night sky. In the poorer farmlands, where people lived by the hours of daylight, it would be pitch-black outside by now, and the only sounds would be the rustling of the wind and the chirping of insects. Here in the city, however, light and the sounds of revelry spilled out onto the streets from the taverns. Adventurers back from hunting and merchants loaded with the day's profits shared stories and cracked jokes over pints of warm ale. In another two hours, even those last vestiges of activity would die out, and the night would be silent, but for now, it was the perfect time to go unnoticed.

We were headed to the walls a little east of the north gate, near the bounds of the slums. The hoods of the robes we had picked up at the clothes shop hid our faces as we moved through the night, and we only dropped them once we arrived at our deserted destination.

"We're here. This is the place," I announced.

I placed my hand gently on the wall and felt its cold stone, robbed of heat by the cool night air. It was as white as marble, but there was something rough like sand mixed in, and the moonlight glinted off its uneven surface. This was a material known as starlite, which had the unique ability to absorb mana from the air. Thanks to the spells cast on it, the wall could use this energy to repair itself.

"Master? I don't see any hole...," murmured Minnalis, examining the wall. Indeed, she could look all she wanted, and she wouldn't find so much as a single scratch mark.

"Well, of course. If it were that obvious, it would have already been patched over. I never said there was a hole already. We need to make one."

"Make one? You mean, break the wall? Apologies, Master, but I don't think—"

To anyone with half a brain, it was common sense that the walls of the capital were indestructible. Children were told in fairy tales that these walls held fast under the charge of an Earth Dragon, a terrifying class-A monster that couldn't fly but had immense strength. Even if that was just a fable, there were surviving records of the walls withstanding attacks from other equally impressive and rare monsters. For a single entity to breach the walls was an absurd notion, unheard of in even the drunkest adventurer's tallest tales.

For the people living within them, the fall of the city walls would spell the end of the world. It was only because they knew the walls would stand firm against any attack that they could sleep soundly at night despite the monsters roaming the forests, plains, mountains, and tundras outside.

Anything with the power to penetrate the walls unaided would be a mythical being, right out of the pages of a children's book.

…Would the people make me a hero, or a monster? Last time, it was the latter.

"A wall is nothing more than a pile of hard stones, Minnalis. How do you suppose it can withstand attacks from the strongest monsters in the world?"

"Well, because it has all sorts of magical enchantments, doesn't it?"

"Correct. All city walls have Self-Repair, Degradation Down, and Hardness Up enchantments. In addition, the walls of the capital have the properties Absorb Shock and Magic Dampen. Those magics have a lot of power invested in them to keep them at a very high level, and that power comes from the starlite, which absorbs mana from the air, that was mixed into these stones."

Of course, all this was top secret information that only the privileged class had access to. As far as the citizenry was aware, it was just "a super-amazing wall that could repel any attack." That was the only thing they needed to know.

"Meaning if it can't get that mana, the wall's strength will drop. It'll just be a normal stone wall. That wouldn't be so hard to break through, would it? And one more thing…"

I grinned and pointed toward the wall with the Soul Blade of Beginnings, a sword with no special abilities save the power to strengthen the blade by channeling mana into it.

"These little creatures eat *more than just mana*."

"Oh…"

I knew the wall was weak, but it crumbled even more easily than

I'd expected. Using the tip of my blade, I tore away a stone, which fell to the ground along with several small translucent maggots of different colors: red, brown, and green. They wriggled on the ground, squeaking, their bodies coated in a transparent mucus that glinted in the moonlight.

And there, in the cavity...

Squirm, squirm.

...the stones were overflowing with maggots, hundreds of them.

Compared with the cool, rough, hard exterior, the inside of the wall was warm and wet with mucus, like looking into a monster's guts. Even the white color had faded to a dull brown.

"Are they eating it?"

"That's right. They're a type of class-D monster known as Magiphages, or Magic Eaters. These are actually a subspecies. They use their special mucus to melt down minerals and consume the mana within. They'll keep feeding and multiplying until the entire wall is nothing but a pile of sand. I know them as Wall Eaters, but to be precise, this subspecies has yet to be discovered, and they *haven't even been officially named yet.*"

The inside of the walls looked completely ruined. The maggots had eaten so many holes into the stonework, it resembled a sponge. They had taken their time, softening it little by little, imperceptibly, until it was so brittle that the slightest touch caused parts of it to disintegrate into dust.

"It's now far weaker than any stone wall. Getting through the hard shell is the most difficult part. After that, it just opens up."

As I poked the tip of my soul blade deeper into the wall, bits of stonework crumbled away along with the squealing Wall Eaters. The deeper I went, the more tightly packed the Wall Eaters became, until it looked more like a wall of flesh than of stone.

"..."

Minnalis just stared, dumbfounded. Even I was having trouble stomaching the idea of putting my hand any nearer to the writhing mass of maggots—thousands upon thousands of see-through little blobs dyed with red, brown, and green streaks like marbles. I wouldn't be surprised if a girl like Minnalis was ready to faint from disgust—

"Master, what if we put one of our enemies in a hole and covered them in these maggots?" she asked with a serious look. It appeared I had underestimated her once again. She kept surpassing my expectations. I wanted to laugh.

"Hmm, not a bad idea, but just covering them is a bit low-level. What if we made them breed, multiply within their body, and devour them from the inside?"

"Impressive, Master. It certainly would be more effective if they felt the pain of being eaten from within."

"Why not both? We could have them eat away from the outside, too. Hmm, no, that's not very interesting. Perhaps if we could cause the skin to rot in some way..."

"Instead of filling their organs with maggots, we could bury the maggots in their skin. Imagine having to pull maggots out of your own skin, but they just keep coming! It could be fun to keep them sane the whole time instead of using my magic to drive them mad like we did today."

"What if we had the dead ones come back to life as zombies and transfer their maggots to the survivors through their mouths? Although, that would mean some of them would have to die early. Maybe that plan needs a little work..."

We seemed to have gotten sidetracked into some sort of impromptu brainstorming session. Two heads really were better than one, and getting another person's perspective was good stimulation for the brain.

As we chatted happily about our macabre subject, the tip of my soul blade opened up a hole in the wall that was large enough for a horse to pass through. The ground was littered with sliced and trampled Wall Eaters, which were lying in a puddle of slime and the crumbling remnants of the stone wall.

"Master, was it you who put these maggots here?"

"I wish I could say that it was, but no. I'd never even seen them until now. Anyway, look, we can get through."

The tunnel in the wall reminded me of a hole in a sandpit. When we passed through it, we found ourselves in a thick forest. The moonlight filtering through the trees lent an air of mystery to the eerie environment.

"Yep, there's no saving it now," I muttered to myself. I gave a sigh of relief now that we were finally out of the city. Over the last year, I had come to feel that it was safer outside the walls than within them. I wondered if this was how criminals felt.

"Oh, almost forgot," I said, heading back inside the walls. I scavenged up whatever I could find and dropped it in front of the fresh opening.

"Master, let me help," declared Minnalis. "You're trying to conceal the hole, right?"

"Hmm? Ah, thanks. Try not to wake anyone up, though."

The wall wasn't supposed to collapse for another few days. If they found out now, they might still be able to *contain* the damage. Besides, I already knew how things went down the first time. Why not try to *spice it up* the second time around?

"It's a bit silly of me to ask after lugging all this trash around, but do you think you could cast an illusion on the hole to hide it?"

"...Sorry, Master, but I'm a beastfolk. I can keep refreshing the illusions cast on myself as much as I like, but even if I leave one here, I don't think it would last much longer than a day at most. I suppose if I kept coming back to recast it..."

"Forget it. We don't have time to stick around. This cover should be more than enough to fool the people around here anyway."

I sneered at the townspeople, who by now were in their beds. This place was on the brink of becoming part of the slums. Nobody would notice if a single pile of trash was out of place the next morning. People were too busy with their lives. All they cared about here was staying above the poverty line, and they'd sell their closest confidant if they thought it would help.

The longer they remained ignorant, the worse the infestation in the walls would grow.

"Well, seeing how many we killed getting through the hole, *the least we could do* to make up for it is give them a little extra time to eat the walls, don't you think?"

"You're right, Master. Why, these maggots are practically saints compared with the scum who live here. Ohhh, I just want to strangle the lot of them to death right now!"

"Unfortunately, I don't think we have time for that. Just find solace in the fact that thanks to *this*, a few of them will end up dying horrible deaths."

At length, we finished our makeshift cover. Nobody would ever spot any trace of the hole in the wall unless they specifically came over and moved the trash out of the way.

"Oh, here's an idea. Let's take some of these guys with us."

I scooped up several of the Wall Eaters that were still alive into a glass bottle. Then I piled up some twigs and leaves to cover up the hole in the wall from the outside, too.

"Right. Let's start by heading a little deeper into the woods. There's an abandoned hunters' lodge up ahead."

"Okay, Master."

I was quite familiar with the topography of the surrounding woodlands from my first time here. I knew exactly which way to go.

"Once we're there, we can plan our next move. First, we need to get rid of your Weak status. It's a shame for a girl as beautiful as you to be walking around with her stats halved."

It was handy having a pretty girl around. In battle or negotiations, that sort of thing mattered more often than you might think. There had even been a time where I was forced to disguise myself as a woman using my soul blades, though I wished I could banish those memories from my brain.

Anyway, forget about that. This time, I had Minnalis, who as anyone could see was gorgeous, and she'd be even better-looking once she had a decent meal and some good rest.

"F-flattery will get you nowhere, Master. You don't need to butter me up to get anything out of me. I am your slave, after all."

"I'm not trying to get anything out of you. Don't treat me like a playboy."

"A playboy? What's a playboy?"

Minnalis appeared a little red-faced as she puzzled over my words. I thought she might still be feeling a little of the MP drunkenness, but maybe this was just how she reacted to compliments. Putting that aside, I pondered how best to answer her question.

"Aaah, like a player... How can I explain it? It's like, oh, I don't know..."

The two of us walked deeper into the forest together as the moon shone high above us.

*　　*　　*

"Haaah!"

"Gaaaaagh!"

I felt flesh and bone part under my blade, and the boar-like monster gave a cry of pain as it died. I say *boar-like*, but its green fur and the single black horn atop its head made it pretty difficult to mistake it for the real thing.

It was a beast-type monster known as a Green Boar—a regular foe for beginner adventurers, roughly on the same level as a goblin, though rarer. (It would be fairer to say that goblins were freakishly common.) While the boar's attacks were slightly stronger than those of a goblin, it could only charge in a straight line, which made them easy pickings.

The most important distinction, however, was that you could eat them. It was about the worst-quality meat you could get, but it filled the stomach, and it was incredibly common for poorer adventurers who were just starting out to keep dried pork on them as emergency rations.

"Gragh! Gah!"

I sliced past the Green Boar, taking out its right foreleg before delivering the finishing blow by cleanly lopping off its head with the Soul Blade of Beginnings. I was tempted to hang it up on a tree from its hind legs to drain out every bit of blood, but we had all the meat we needed, and so I left its body on the forest floor. It would only take a few hours for a pack of garm, a type of canine monster, to show up, attracted by the smell. Their intelligence was low, and they would likely feast on the Green Boar without bothering to check their surroundings. The plan was to ambush them from behind while they were distracted and reap a load of experience points in the process.

"*Phew*, finally above three thousand…"

I was retracing my steps to where Minnalis was waiting, checking my experience using my status screen. It had been two days since we escaped from the city together, and I had spent that time hunting goblins, Green Boars, and garm to raise my level and improve my combat ability.

The knights I'd encountered in the summoning chamber were weak, with most of them never having seen actual combat in their lives. They were mostly for ceremony, to lend an air of respectability to the castle. I could hold my own against a group twice their size, but the combat squad led by the royal-knight commander was a different story.

The ceremonial knights held their posts only because they were the sons of nobility, and they worked to increase their levels in relative safety, surrounded by their squires. Their main purpose was to instill a sense of respect and admiration in the people.

Meanwhile, the combat squad existed only for battle. When war broke out or monsters attacked, and invaders slipped through the gates, the royal combat squad put their lives on the line to defend the kingdom. Some of them were so grizzled and scarred that the kingdom was hesitant to put them on display. Their skills, however, were real.

If I got surrounded by more than about a dozen of them, I'd have no choice but to run. Otherwise, they'd hang my body from the castle walls for all to see.

I could spend my experience points either on raising my level or unlocking my soul blades. The priority was getting my power back as quickly as possible.

"Seriously, Goddess. This negative twenty thousand is a hefty penalty..." I let out a long sigh.

I had killed a grand total of fifty-four goblins, Green Boars, and garm over the past two days and gained about two thousand experience points. Even added to the points I still hadn't spent yet, everything came up to only three thousand. Twenty thousand was still a long way off. What's more, I had been pretty lucky at spotting groups of monsters so far, and I didn't expect this pace to continue.

"'New Game Plus,' my ass… This is even harder than last time."

The monsters near the capital were weak, with an average level of around 20. That was about the same as an adult male who lived and worked in the city and never set foot beyond its walls. However, having the same level didn't mean they were of the same combat potential. Monsters had higher stats, and their instincts were geared for battle. In a head-to-head showdown between a human and a goblin of the same level, the goblin would win every time.

For experience, it was stats that made the difference, not level. You wouldn't get much experience from an enemy with weaker stats than you, no matter how high their level was compared with yours. I might be level 1, but I was being buffed by my soul blades, and, although I couldn't check right now, my *titles*. All in all, they were giving me about fifty levels' worth of stat boosts. Monsters might be stronger than humans on average, but these ones were way weaker than me.

"We can save leveling up for later. Let's start by unlocking the Eight-Eyed Sword of Clarity."

I brought up my status screen, went to my soul-blade display, and tapped its name.

Eight-Eyed Sword of Clarity
Unlock Condition: Use any soul blade to sever the Eight-Eyed Crystal, which is said to see through any deception.

Effect: Gain the ability to use Appraise to retrieve more detailed information about your target.

Once obtained, any information discovered using Appraise can be read at your leisure.

Also allows you to see the status screen of any individual.

Passive Effect:
+50 Resistance
Experience Required to Unlock:
0/3,000
Available Experience: 3,011

After allotting the required experience points, I closed the window and conjured the Eight-Eyed Sword of Clarity. It was a short survival knife that fit neatly in my hand. The blade was slightly curved, and the opposite edge was cut with tiny serrations. Eight round holes, each about the size of my thumb, were scattered across the thick part of the blade, and in every one of the holes was a crystal: seven colors of the rainbow, and the eighth a jet-black. At the base of the handle, there was a crystal containing an image of a book, which was set in a ring of gold. When the ring was twisted a quarter turn, the image changed from a closed book to an open one, and a green transparent window appeared that was not unlike a status screen. This one was called a data board.

"Huh. Looks like I still have the data from last time."

Appraisal Records: Monsters   Search _____

- -

Goblin Types:

    Goblin

    Sword Goblin

    Archer Goblin

    Magic Goblin

    Monk Goblin

    Sage Goblin

    Red Goblin

    Blue Goblin

    Yellow Goblin

    Green Goblin

    Blood Goblin

    Needle Goblin

    Muscle Goblin

    Trash Goblin

    ....

    ....

    ......

Just to confirm, I checked my item info as well, and sure enough, the details of the items I had encountered the previous time were all still there. I closed the data board by twisting the ring back and tied the knife to my belt. I needed to have the blade summoned to use Appraise, and since it didn't cost MP to have out, I usually carried it around with me.

"Open Status. Appraise."

The next step was to use Appraise on my own status screen. That caused a green data board to appear over my blue status screen.

Kaito Ukei

Hidden Statistics:

Finesse: SSS

Reaction Time: SS

Recovery Rate: F

Status: OK

Magic Affinity:

Fire: 0	Light: 0
Water: 0	Dark: 0
Wind: 0	Null: 0
Earth: 0	Misc.: 0

Acquired Titles:

Otherworlder, Hero, Soul-Blade Bearer,

Fleetest of Foot, Adamant Iron Wall,

Vanquisher of Evil, Enemy of the World,

Master of Finesse, Fugitive, Vower of

Vengeance, Avenger's Master

Now that we've seen all the various status pages, let's go over the stats.

HP

Hit Points. This value represents a person's health. Taking damage can cause it to go down, as can poison or disease. If this value drops to zero, you die.

MP

Magic Points. Shows how much mana resides in your body. Casting magic, as well as certain skills, such as "Intimidate" and "Mana Blade," can cause this value to drop.

Strength

Indicates the maximum physical power a person can exert.

Stamina

Indicates the extent to which a person can continuously exert themselves.

Vitality

Affects the amount of damage taken from attacks.

Dexterity

Indicates the maximum speed at which a person can move.

Magic

Affects the extent to which using more mana than needed improves the effects of spells or skills.

Resistance

Affects the amount of damage taken from magical attacks or effects.

* * *

These were all the stats that appeared on a normal status screen. You couldn't just look at another person's screen, but everyone could see their own and show them to other people if they so wished. I was only allowed to see Minnalis's screen because of my Avenger's Master title; even purchasing her as a slave hadn't granted me that permission.

However, what the people of this world didn't know was that there were other stats being tracked. Those hidden stats were what my data board was currently showing me. Unlike normal stats, these hidden stats didn't have numbers but were instead ranked on a letter scale from G up to SSS. I'll explain them next.

Finesse

This grade indicates physical control over one's body, and the extent to which a person can leverage the numerical values of their stats.

Reaction Time

The speed at which you can process information obtained through one's senses, skills, and magic. This grade also indicates how fast a person can think in battle.

Recovery Rate

Indicates the speed at which HP and MP recover. Also influences the recovery speed of status conditions, as well as damaged or missing body parts.

These statistics were only visible to me thanks to the effect of the Eight-Eyed Sword of Clarity. Even spells with the Appraise effect didn't show them. As for the Magic Affinities, it was possible to estimate their values using special Affinity Crystals that were produced and sold by the Magicians' Guild. However, these were quite expensive, so most people didn't know their Affinities at all.

These Affinities indicated one's aptitude for a particular class of magic. People with high Affinity found it easier to cast advanced spells and also raised the level of their skill faster. So for a Fire mage, that would be their "Fire Magic" skill.

Incidentally, "Null" magic referred to support spells like Force Up and Physical Up, while "Misc." magic contained exotic spells, such as curses, illusions, spirit magic, and rituals, that fell outside the usual classifications. Misc. magic also affected spells that combined the effects of multiple categories: Fire, Water, Wind, Earth, Light, Dark, and Null, though to be honest, I didn't fully understand how it worked myself.

These Affinities were more or less set in stone from the moment you were born. Now, I'm sure the eagle-eyed among you have noticed that my Affinities were zero across the board. That's right: I couldn't use magic. I didn't even know how to convert mana into a spell. It wasn't too much of a problem, however. The abilities of my soul blades were rather like spells, and all I had to do was channel mana into them. I didn't have to worry about casting anything. Granted, they tended to use a sizable amount of MP and have dramatic effects, so they weren't the best fit for every situation, but they were similar to spells just in terms of their nature and structure.

Finally, there were my titles. There were parts to the title system that I didn't quite understand yet, but as far as I could tell, they were like passive skills in that they were unlocked by satisfying certain conditions and granted different effects. Depending on the title, these effects could vary quite considerably. For example, my "Otherworlder" title granted me the "Auto-Translate" intrinsic ability, while "Hero" sped up the rate at which I gained points in skill proficiency.

As for "Master of Finesse," it caused my Finesse to remain at SSS without degrading, even if I failed to train regularly.

Titles were also only visible to me because of the Eight-Eyed Sword of Clarity, and basically, no one else even knew they existed. On top of that, their unlock conditions were invisible, and they were even harder to obtain than skills, so very few people possessed even a single title.

"They're all still there, too..."

I hadn't been sure until now, but my stats had seemed to be higher than just what my soul blades accounted for. As such, I'd suspected my titles had been similarly preserved, and I was right.

Satisfied with my findings, I closed the data board just as I arrived back at the hunting lodge.

"Ah, Master, you're back!" exclaimed Minnalis at my arrival, wiping the sweat from her brow.

"...Hey, didn't I tell you to get some sleep?" I asked, frowning.

The bunny girl was busy swinging her sword in the front yard. Apparently, it was too much for her rabbit brain to remember what I had told her that very morning. Right now, there was nobody around, and so she had let her illusion come undone, revealing her soft ears and fluffy tail.

"I'm okay now, Master. My Weak condition wore off about an hour ago. Besides, it's going to be worse for me if I stay cooped up in bed all day," she said nonchalantly. She did appear to be in much better health.

I decided to see for myself using my new Appraise ability. As a beastfolk, she indeed had a fast Recovery Rate.

Minnalis

Hidden Statistics:

Finesse: F

Reaction Time: E

Recovery Rate: D

Status: OK

Magic Affinity:

Fire: 20   Light: 89

Water: 61   Dark: 85

Wind: 22   Null: 38

Earth: 11   Misc.: 118

Acquired Titles:

Slave to Revenge,

Bearer of Intoxicating Phantasm,

Remaker of Life

Incidentally, it was possible to raise one's Recovery Rate by using magic or skills, but even a combat-hardened veteran typically had a grade of only around E.

"Looks like your Weakness really has gone," I observed.

I also noticed that her Affinities for Light, Dark, and Misc. magic were remarkably high. Most people became wizards if their score was above forty. If beastfolk magic wasn't so bad at long-range attacks, she would make for excellent magical artillery. However, the drawback persisted even when a beastfolk's mana was converted into a spell, so that plan was a dud.

"Fine, whatever," I said. "Let's have some food."

"Yes, Master. I've already taken the liberty of making something."

"Ah, thanks."

"No need to thank me. I'm your slave, after all."

I headed inside the hunter's lodge with Minnalis. She used to blush with embarrassment when she was affected by MP drunkenness, but now she seemed to take my gratitude in stride. (I refused to think it was because she was already getting sick of my praise.)

Inside were two beds (though the second was simply a piece of cloth, placed over the area where hunters used to pile their catches), a small table, and a fireplace. When we first arrived two days ago, the place had been covered in a thick layer of dust, and it was obvious that it had not been used in some time. After giving the area a quick clean, I had put Minnalis to bed, her Weakness relief potion having worn off, and focused on getting her food and rest. Now she was even looking fuller around the face and limbs, a testament to the fast recovery speed of beastfolk. Her hair and skin were looking more luscious than ever, and her eyes were big and bright again. Only her chest size had not returned to normal (though she was still obviously well-endowed), and she appeared to be a little down about it.

But the past few days had also affected her desire for revenge.

When we made our pact and witnessed each other's memories, we had only seen an abridged version of sorts. We had a general idea of what had happened, and we felt what the other had felt, but we didn't know any of the details of the events that had led up to that point. The first thing I'd asked Minnalis when I had the chance was exactly whom she wanted to get revenge on and why.

The girl she'd saved stabbed her in the back. People she'd thought she could rely on turned against her. I had expected that different people would still want revenge for similar reasons, but some of those reasons struck far closer to home than I had thought they would, and listening to her talk made me feel sick to my stomach. I didn't say a word; I just listened. Even when she was done, I didn't say anything. I didn't tell her it must have been tough. I didn't tell her she was right to feel that way. I didn't offer her a single word of consolation.

Offering words of pity was the same as tossing down contempt from on high. Even if you said them with the best of intentions, they could still hurt. People who truly sympathized knew just how humiliating it was to be pitied, and they kept those words to themselves. The only people who could speak them aloud were those who had never been burned by this heat.

Furthermore, Minnalis's revenge was my revenge now, and the time for self-pity was long gone by this point.

Last night, Minnalis finished recounting up to where we met. Then it was my turn to tell her my story. How I was a hero summoned from another world. How I had lived through this world once already, been betrayed by the princess and the rest of my companions, and sworn revenge against them. And how I had been reborn into the summoning chamber and disabled the princess and her guards before making my escape.

From my brief summary, Minnalis only really half understood what I had been through, but having lived through some of it, and with me reexplaining some parts to her, she finally seemed to get it. When I stopped to think about it, it was pretty impressive that a normal village girl like Minnalis could even read and write. (Supposedly, she had learned from the merchant caravans that frequented the village.)

Minnalis seemed like quite a shrewd girl by this world's standards. She was pretty, smart, and athletic. Back on Earth, a girl like this would have been way out of my league. By what miracle was she my partner in crime now?

"Master, be sure to eat. Your food's getting cold."

"Oh, yeah."

At some point while I was lost in reflection, sitting on a cut log with my head in my hands, a bowl of soup had appeared before me. It contained Green Boar meat with dried vegetables. Steam was rising from the salty broth, and it seemed delicious. At least, it looked better than anything I could make.

"Huh? Where did you get these spoons?"

I had only packed forks when I was in town, yet on the table beside our bowls, there was a pair of wooden spoons.

"I whittled them out of a wooden branch. I thought it would be easier to eat with a spoon."

Sure enough, some of the meat and vegetables were cut pretty finely. A fork wouldn't be optimal here.

"Wow, that's impressive," I praised. "Did you use to do this kind of thing back at the village, too?"

"Yes. In winter, I would make wooden sculptures to help with the family finances. I don't think these are very good, though. I might redo them later."

"I see. They seem pretty fine to me."

I wasn't sure why Minnalis was unsatisfied with them, but she was the expert. If she thought they were lacking, then there wasn't much I could say to convince her. I took a spoon and began to eat.

"I hope you like it. How does it taste?"

"Mmm. It's good. You're a pretty good cook, Minnalis."

Thinking back, the food she had prepared the day we first met had looked pretty tasty, too. You know, if it hadn't been filled with goblin-transformation serum and monster poison.

"Thank you. That was delicious," I said, placing my hands together.

"I'm glad to see you liked it, but, er, Master, why are you praying...?"

"Oh, that's just something people did in my world."

When I said that, Minnalis's expression grew uncertain.

"Master, do you...? Are you going to go back to your world one day?"

"Oh, don't worry. I'm not about to leave you high and dry without letting you fulfill your revenge."

Minnalis appeared a little relieved by my words.

"And also...I think even after I get my revenge, when I calm down, when I'm able to take my time and search for a way back... I don't think I'll ever return. It's too late. There's nothing for me there."

After I emptied my thoughts, I stood up and took our bowls from the table.

"Anyway, we don't need to think about that until our revenge is over. Let's deal with the problems in front of us for now."

"Master, I'll clean the dishes. Please sit down."

"The first thing we have to do is build up our strength."

"Master, I'll clean the dishes. Please sit down."

"...Er, Minnalis? Are you listening to me?"

"Master, I'll clean the dishes. Please sit down."

"..."

My casual smile was beaten back by the sudden and strange intensity of Minnalis's bearing as she stubbornly repeated her words with both arms outstretched. Was the uneasiness I thought I saw flash across her face just an illusion?

"Master. I'll clean the dishes."

She spoke slowly, her face never breaking from her perfect smile. I was unsure what was driving her, but I handed over the bowls. She nodded once happily and drew them close to her chest.

"And then? What specifically were you planning we do next, Master?"

"Oh, er…"

It was like nothing had even happened, but it had unsettled me enough for me to lose my train of thought, so I cleared my throat and started again.

"Er, well, ten days from now, I was planning to enter a dungeon a short way from here. It hasn't been discovered yet, you see. Then we're going to *kill all the monsters inside.*"

A beat passed as the air in the hut was silent, before Minnalis emitted a small sound.

"…Huh?"

Several kilometers northeast from the hunter's lodge was a cave. When the dungeon appeared there, a rockfall sealed off the entrance almost immediately, so nobody had discovered it yet. It was due to be discovered in another month, when an earthquake would reveal the entrance, allowing a veteran adventurer who was out with a group of newbies to come across it.

Dungeons formed following the spontaneous appearance of something called a Dungeon Core, a metal sphere with golem-like qualities that warped the surrounding environment into a labyrinth. Monsters appeared more frequently inside them, and over time, the dungeons grew larger, and the monsters within more powerful and more plentiful.

The Dungeon Core remained within the labyrinth's depths, defended by a formidable monster known as a Guardian, which wielded powerful equipment created using the dungeon's magic. If the Dungeon Core was destroyed, the magic was dispelled, and the dungeon became an inert tangle of passages and rooms.

Compared with all the dungeons spread across the lands, this one was quite *young*. If it were a human, it would be little more than a baby.

There was no sunlight in cave dungeons, but they were lit by a substance called brightmoss, which lined the walls. There were air vents, too, so adventurers didn't suffocate deeper in. The problem was something we only discovered in the cold, dank depths of the cave network, precisely eight days after arriving.

"Tch! Haaaah!"

"Gaaaaaaargh!"

Steel and steel clashed once more, but the long battle was at last drawing to a close. A single well-placed slice severed the Sword Goblin's hand, which was still wielding its rusty blade. Minnalis leveled her weapon, and as the goblin stepped back in retreat, she lunged forward, placing her longsword right between the goblin's ribs. She was onto her seventh sword, and even it was showing signs of disrepair.

"Gah! Graaaaah!"

"Now to end it!"

The goblin cried out in anger and pain just as a single stroke of Minnalis's blade severed its repulsive head from its shoulders. Unable to give even a dying wail, its body slumped down to the ground, spraying forth gushes of green blood.

"*Phew...* Ah!"

Suddenly, an arrow flew toward Minnalis. Something had been

waiting for the right moment to attack. It was too late to dodge, and she twisted her body so that it might at least miss her vitals.

"That's why I said never to let down your guard."

Using Fleet-Foot to step in quickly, I deflected the arrow upward slightly with my blade so that it missed its target. Some distance away, behind a rocky outcrop, I spotted an Archer Goblin preparing to fire a second arrow.

"I'll let you deal with those wolves for a while."

"O-okay!"

The half dozen or so Gray Garm I had been fighting were perplexed at my sudden disappearance, unable to keep up with the speed of Fleet-Foot. They began to panic, when the howl of a darker-furred individual among them, the Black Garm, caused them to fall into line.

I watched them reorganize out of the corner of my eye before leaving them to Minnalis and heading in a different direction.

"Not on my watch."

With Fleet-Foot, I was able to reach the goblin before it fired its second arrow and cleaved it in two with a single swing of my sword.

"Gaaaah!"

"Be quiet."

I immediately swung my sword back up to take out another goblin, then seconds later, an enormous slab of metal came crashing down, throwing out sparks as I blocked it. It was the monstrous blade of the Highsword Goblin that had been hiding in the shadows, commanding its squad of about a dozen smaller goblins.

"Gaaaargh!"

The goblin bellowed an angry roar at my meddling. It was roughly the same shape as a normal goblin but was bulging with muscles and stood nearly two hundred twenty centimeters tall, twice the size of the rest of its kin.

"I can smell your rage. Though, I guess if you were trying to sneak attack me, that roar would have given you away first."

"Gaaaah! Graaaaagh!"

My intrinsic ability, Auto-Translate, allowed me to understand and be understood by others. However, it only worked on races similar to my own. I could speak with beastfolk, elves, and demons, but not nonhumanoids, even though certain classes of monsters such as beasts and insects could communicate with others of their type.

It was likewise with the goblin in front of me. It couldn't understand what I was saying. Still, it appeared to get that I was making fun of it, and so with a tremendous roar, it swung its enormous sword at mine again, blasting me back.

"Grrr, what a brute…!" I yelled, taken aback by its overwhelming strength.

I used Air Step to correct my posture in midair before glancing over in Minnalis's direction. She was still engaging the Gray Garm in combat, inflicting damage little by little while trying not to let herself be surrounded. It appeared she had grasped the basics of battle strategy very well indeed.

I couldn't afford to slip up here while Minnalis was fighting so bravely. Now that I was some distance from my attacker, I looked at its status to figure out the source of its incredible strength. When I saw what was written on its status screen, I understood.

"Its condition says *OK* and *Cursed*. That means it must have a cursed weapon."

It seemed unlikely that the tattered cloth around the goblin's loins was the source of its power, so I turned my Appraise ability on its greatsword. As I had guessed, the item appeared to be a cursed sword. It was a weapon geared for brute force, well suited to goblins,

Highsword Goblin Lv77

Male • Monster

HP: 1,121/1,212   MP: 256/256 (511)

Strength: 1,321 (521)   Stamina: 524

Vitality: 347 (695)   Dexterity: 527

Magic: 0   Resistance: 248 (497)

Intrinsic Abilities: None

Skills: Sword Lv 4, Greatsword Lv 3 (Granted)

Status: OK Cursed

Greatsword of Grief

A greatsword cursed with the grudges of many a swordsman.

Its wielder becomes unable to do anything but swing this sword with overwhelming strength.

Passive Effect:

+800 Strength, -50% MP, -100% Magic, -50% Vitality, -50% Resistance, Grants Greatsword Lv 3.

which rarely used magic in battle. It was probably by obtaining this sword that the creature evolved from a mere Sword Goblin into a Highsword Goblin.

"What a pain—this thing's not even the dungeon boss, and yet it's so strong."

Cursed weapons were relatively rare, and I had encountered so few over the four years I'd traveled this world that I could count them on one hand. They granted enormous power, but at great cost. The effects alone made them very difficult to use, but as if that weren't bad enough, cursed weapons also had wills of their own and could *devour* the minds of wielders they deemed unsuitable, causing the users to lose their minds and do nothing but rampage wildly.

In that sense, it seemed to consider the goblin a suitable host. The fact that its status said *OK* meant that its soul hadn't yet been fully devoured. That was clear from the way it still acted rationally, but its movements were being guided by the blade.

"Gaaaaaargh!"

"Ugh, this is gonna suck."

I'd fought enemies with cursed weapons before, but I never really struggled. They were weak to the holy magic of the priestess, and I could pick good soul blades to deal with them, not to mention I was much stronger back then. Things were different now. That priestess was one of my sworn enemies, and I hadn't unlocked my more powerful soul blades yet. Facing this foe head-on was a bad idea.

"Gaaaaargh!"

"Hup! Hah… Hup!"

I moved my soul blade and sidestepped the incoming blow. As it swung again, I delivered a quick slice to weaken its next strike. Thankfully, my Finesse and Reaction Time stats were much higher this time around, which helped plug the frightening gap between our levels. However, its stats didn't show me a weakness that was glaring enough for me to take advantage of. Unless I could deliver a decisive blow, this battle was going to keep dragging on.

Then I realized something.

"...I guess I'll give it a try."

I kept on parrying its blows, blunting its attacks, and watching its rage build. Then as it geared up for a big swing, I leaped backward and put some space between us. Despite the frugal use of my MP so far, it had gotten quite low, so I used the time to swig a potion and restore it to full. Then I dismissed the Soul Blade of Beginnings and summoned the Pyrachnid's Claw of Kindling.

The goblin grew ever angrier that none of its attacks were inflicting any serious damage on me. However, when it saw me apparently switch from a longsword to a shorter one, it grinned a sickening smile and pressed the attack once more.

"Gyaaaawaaaargh!"

Closing in on me, the goblin delivered a devastating upward blow. I took a single step to the side, letting the blade pass me by as the air pressure caused my hair to flutter. The goblin then brought its greatsword down on me as a follow-up attack, and there, I stepped in and caught the weapon on the Pyrachnid's Claw.

"Grrr..."

"Gah... Graaaaagh!"

The goblin let out a deafening roar as our two swords clashed. We were going through the same motions as before, but this time, I wouldn't let it blast me back.

"Gragh?"

"Looks like it works. This thing sure is coming in handy a lot."

I can't believe I'd never thought of this tactic before. The goblin's cursed sword...was *metal*.

At the point where our two blades touched, mine was slowly melting through its weapon. It had cut nearly halfway through when the goblin realized something strange was going on and tried to pull its sword away, but by then, it was *too late*.

"...Rargh!"

Grinning, I let go of my soul blade and crafted a midair platform with Air Step. I leaped off it as if to perform a triangle kick, then swung my leg downward, channeling all my mana into my foot and using the force of gravity to bring my heel down onto the broad side of the goblin's greatsword.

"Gaaaargh?!"

There was a dull metallic ring as the cursed sword split into two pieces. The goblin looked at the broken half of the weapon in its hands, dumbfounded. It seemed it hadn't even entertained the possibility that its sword could fail it.

"Now you're wide-open," I snarled.

"Gah... Gragh..."

I wasn't about to give up my advantage, so I quickly switched back to the Soul Blade of Beginnings, channeled a fair bit of mana into it, and swung it, attempting to close out the battle in a single hit. A great gash appeared in the goblin's throat, and the life drained out of it before it fell backward onto the ground. The goblin's fist clasped the sword's hilt so tightly that even in death, it did not release it. The shattered fragments of the blade lay strewed across the floor.

"...*Phew.*"

Without letting down my guard, I checked on Minnalis, but she seemed to be closing out her fight as well. The remnants of the pack littered the floor around her, writhing and whimpering in pain from the many wounds they had taken from her poison-coated blade. The only one still standing was the leader, the Black Garm, and it looked like it would soon fall, too. Minnalis didn't let down her guard, but neither did she change her strategy, and she continued to focus on defense while harassing the Black Garm with multiple tiny cuts loaded with venom.

"Tee-hee! Now dance for me, wolf! Hee-hee! Hee-hee-hee!"

"...Wait, she's not being cautious," I corrected myself. "She's just toying with it. She's used too much of that Intoxicating Phantasm again."

I suppose it was a direct consequence of her fighting so cautiously, but the protracted clash had drained her MP and caused her to suffer inebriation once more. Her sense had gone right out the window, and she was driven only by a lust for battle. Perhaps Minnalis was one of those people it affected quite easily. Her fighting spirit had transformed into pure sadism.

"Come, now. Let me hear those whimpers. Succumb to the poison in your veins... Oh, Master! What did you do that for?"

"I know you won't listen to me, but you need to cool off." I gave a long sigh as I pierced the barely moving Black Garm's body, pinning it to the ground with my sword.

"It's not nice to kill steal. You gotta make it up to me with a kiss! A kiss!"

"Stop babbling like an idiot and finish the job before it gets up. It's not dead yet."

"Urgh... Fine."

I held back Minnalis at arm's length until I felt her give up. The many Gray Garm that made up the pack had already succumbed to the poison and died. Minnalis swung her sword above her head and decapitated the Black Garm, bringing the battle to a close.

"Here, have an MP potion."

"Aren't you gonna feed it to me? Mouth...to...mouth?"

"..."

"Ugh! Ng...ng..."

Ignoring Minnalis's fluttering eyelashes and weird flirtatious behavior, I forced the potion down her throat. It should only take a few minutes before she switched classes back to "Cool Minnalis." She was getting used to the feeling of drunkenness, and as soon as she got out of battle and restored her MP, she would be pretty much normal.

"Paaah! Mmm...this method isn't too bad, either!"

"Whatever. You need a rest. Leave the skinning to me."

I ignored whatever she was talking about and took my newest soul blade, the Squirrel's Blade of Holding, from my belt. This one didn't look remotely suited to cutting at all. It was only about fifty centimeters long, including the hilt, with brown fur all over the blade part and nothing to call an edge; it was more of a furry tube that flopped about like its bones were missing. It functioned as an item box of sorts. While it lowered my maximum MP by 5 percent, it allowed me to stow an infinite number of items.

Most soul blades, if I attempted to give them to someone else, would disappear and return inside me, but this sword didn't do that. As long as they paid the price, anyone I allowed to could take it with them. Minnalis had thus paid 5 percent of her maximum MP as well, so that we could share it.

By channeling mana into the Squirrel's Blade of Holding, the bit of it that was supposed to be the blade swelled up like a balloon, and an opening appeared along the side. In this state, I could leave it on the ground and take out my skinning knife, which I'd bought at the item shop. Recalling my memories from the first time around, I located the prized parts of monsters and any usable materials and threw them into the bag-like sword. Dead monsters would soon be swallowed up by the dungeon itself, so I had to work quickly. I also didn't want a pack of monsters to ambush us and force us to fight with worn-out tools.

"Let's take this with us, too."

I looked down at the two halves of the Highsword Goblin's cursed weapon, the Greatsword of Grief, and threw both pieces into the bag. Just as I was finishing my looting, the first of the monsters' dead bodies sank into the ground. I returned to Minnalis to find that her high had worn off, and she was no longer in that weird sexual mood of hers.

"I'm sorry, Master. You must be so disappointed in me."

"It's fine, and it looked like you fought sensibly enough. It sure was tiring taking on two groups at once, though."

With that, I approached the rock that Minnalis was sitting on and sat down beside her. We only originally intended to battle the garm pack and had lured them to this rocky location so that Minnalis could practice combat with lots of natural obstacles around. Then just as we started fighting, the goblins showed up from a different entrance.

The monsters within dungeons always prioritized attacking humanoids if any were around, rather than one another. If other monsters were nearby, they might even join forces if their rapport was good enough. Goblins and garm shared one such relationship. In effect, we were fighting on two fronts, which was why we needed to split up.

"Let's break for food," I suggested. "We can head for the Core in the afternoon and finally beat this dungeon. I'm starting to miss the sun."

I took some dried meat and hard rye bread from the Squirrel's Blade of Holding, along with some water. The brightmoss gave off a constant dim glow, day and night, and provided little in the way of heat. Minnalis nodded. Having spent so long trapped inside a small cage, she probably felt the same way. I lifted my canteen, which was made of a leather like oxhide, to my lips and quenched my battle-parched throat. I had filled the canteen using one of the first soul blades I unlocked in this dungeon, the Fairy's Blade of Water.

This soul blade had no blade at all, just a hilt. By channeling mana into the sword or pouring water on it, a sharp, watery blade could be made to appear. I didn't intend to use it as a weapon unless there was water nearby, as my max MP was still quite low. However, I could also channel mana into the sword to produce fresh drinking water. This meant I never had to worry about suffering dehydration or thirst while on a journey.

We had culled ninety-two groups of monsters since entering the dungeon, so it was unlikely we would be attacked anytime soon, but still, there was no sense in dawdling. Minnalis was clearly feeling tired from the eight days we had spent here, too, as she quickly polished off her meal.

"Let's head to the boss room next. We must have killed more or less all the enemies in here by now, and I think I remember how the place is laid out."

It was me and my party who'd cleared out this dungeon the last time, but the past four years had left me quite foggy on some details. It was only after walking around this place for over a week that I was starting to remember the layout. I attempted to take the shortest path to where my vague recollections told me the boss room ought to be, making short work of any goblin or garm attacks we ran into along the way.

Then eventually, we arrived before a massive pair of strange metal doors laid into the stone.

"Is this it, Master...?"

"Yes, this is it. The dungeon's inner sanctum. The Guardian Room."

Minnalis gulped at the oppressive aura the double doors gave off.

"I hear the Guardian is far stronger than any monster to be found elsewhere in the dungeon. Are we really going to fight it?" asked Minnalis, worried.

She was right to be afraid. Normally, clearing a dungeon like this would involve the work of a party of at least six people. Even if you discounted the retainers, whose only job was to carry food and water, a party of two was somewhat lacking. And that was just for the dungeon, not the Guardian. To defeat that, one party typically wasn't enough. It took a dozen strong parties, a flawless plan of attack, every precaution you could think of, countless rehearsals, and rotating the combatants in the front lines, and even then, you had to be willing to suffer losses. That was what dungeon-delving adventurers referred to as a "Guardian Raid."

To fight a Guardian with only two people was either suicidal or mad. Though, I had gotten stupidly powerful last time, and we could usually take on dungeon bosses with a single party of five or six.

"Yeah, we're gonna kill the Guardian. A Dungeon Core is made of a material that's infused with a tremendous amount of mana. We can use it to make super-strong equipment."

Dungeons were an important source of natural resources, and a country that controlled the land where a dungeon appeared would often forbid the destruction of its Core. The Core was what caused the monsters and, thus, the loot to keep appearing, and without it, the dungeon would go barren. That was why we needed to secure this dungeon's Core while the kingdom was still unaware of its existence.

"I see... Master, I urge you to reconsider! If we die here, our revenge will go unfulfilled!"

Minnalis pleaded with me desperately. I gave her a playful poke on the forehead.

"Calm down, silly. I never said we'd attack it head-on. I don't want to get myself killed, either. If we took it on in a fair fight, I'd say our chances were about fifty-fifty. I want that Core, but those odds are a no go."

"Well then...er... What...?"

"I guess I should have told you this earlier. The Dungeon grants the Guardian powerful equipment, but it also dominates its mind and forces it to protect the Core. That means it can't leave that room, and if we attack it from outside, it can't fight back."

"From outside? But I heard that when you open the doors, it comes out to this area in front."

"Yes, that's right. We know the Guardian will follow you out here if you let it. We also know that if you close the door, it won't come after you until you open the door again. That means *we have to kill it with the door closed.*"

I drew the Pyrachnid's Claw of Kindling and channeled mana into it.

"From outside... Ahhh, I see. Good idea, Master."

"Well, I'm not even sure if this'll work. If not, we'll just have to give up. We got most of what we came here for: experience points and teaching you how to fight."

When the kingdom was your enemy, you never knew when and where somebody could turn against you. The best way to learn how to defend against any attack was to throw yourself into the fray, and right now, when we needed to lay low, this was the best place to do that.

"We don't need to take any risks against this guy. Even if all we get is his experience points, that's good enough."

Saying that, I started to melt off a portion of the metal door. It was as tough as a boss-room door should be, even harder to cut through than that cursed greatsword.

"I'll cut a hole into the door, then you can use your Intoxicating Phantasm to fill the room with long-lasting poison fumes. Oh, and one other thing. While I doubt the Guardian will start moving before it sees us, try to make it invisible and scentless, too."

After telling Minnalis the plan, I turned my attention back to my soul blade, which was still having trouble cutting through the steel door, and channeled even more mana into it. The blade suddenly sank into the metal, and I pulled it back to reveal a small hole about five centimeters long.

"Okay. That should…do…it…?"

Suddenly, the world started spinning. Part of me realized, *Oh, MP withdrawal*, but it all so quickly started to feel unimportant.

"Sorry…Minnalis… You handle…the rest… I'm sure it'll be fine… I'm just gonna take a short break."

Summoning up the last vestiges of my sensible mind, I turned my back to the wall and slumped down to the ground so I wouldn't make a fool of myself. The Guardian couldn't come out while the door was closed, after all, and no monsters ever went near the entrance to the boss room. The entrance to the dungeon, too, was hidden by stones.

"Yes, Master. I will finish the job. You just rest."

I watched as Minnalis poured some water on the hole I had burned through the door to cool it. She then used her Intoxicating Phantasm to summon up a cloud of poisonous smoke, which she released into the hole.

If she just used normal poison magic, it wouldn't travel very far before dispersing because of her beastfolk heritage. The poison she created with her intrinsic ability wasn't affected by that, though. As far as I understood it, Intoxicating Phantasm allowed her to create magical poisons with a variety of effects. These poisons also never went away on their own and could only be dispelled when the caster willed it. There were supposedly other effects, too, but I hadn't gotten around to learning them yet. When I used Appraise, I could see that these other effects existed, but they had ??????????? listed in place of a name. Intoxicating Phantasm had levels like a skill; it could be improved, and further effects unlocked, by satisfying certain conditions or improving certain skills. Perhaps, as the name implied, it had effects related to illusions...

That was about as far as I got before my mind started to drift and I was overcome with an unbearable weariness. I could feel the drunkenness causing my muscles, which were already strained from the prolonged fighting, to relax. Then without even giving me the chance to resist, my mind was pulled into the inky depths of unconsciousness like a stone drifting to the bottom of the sea.

CHAPTER 5
The Hero's Nightmare

H ey, have you heard? They say the hero made some kinda deal with devils, and by killing the demon lord, he's all set up to take her place. Turns out he ain't as goody two-shoes as he led us to believe."

"Yeah, I heard that. Also heard he was behind the rebellion in the slums. Apparently, he went to the king after that and told him to enslave the whole lot of 'em. The king couldn't say no, poor devil."

"Guess now that he's the new demon lord, he's forgotten who helped him get this far. I mean, the slum dwellers aren't *all* criminals—most of 'em are just people who can't afford to eat no more, now that everything's so damn expensive. That hero's a real asshole."

"Yeah, he doesn't deserve to be called a hero. He makes me sick."

In the royal capital was a run-down tavern a little off the high street. The sky outside was gloomy and gray, and rain hit the ground like buckets of water.

Damn them, talking shit behind my back...

I sipped my watered-down ale and listened closer to the surrounding voices, my hood pulled low over my face to conceal my identity. However, all they did was complain about how they couldn't go hunting because of the rain, or about how their wives wouldn't let them spend any money. I wasn't drunk yet, but my thoughts started to turn introspective.

...It had been nearly six months since I defeated the demon lord. Everywhere I went, my reputation was in the gutter, and the deeds I'd supposedly done got worse every day. Even here in the royal capital, where I'd spent so many of my days, I was an outlaw. The times I had once been lauded as a savior seemed so far away.

I couldn't even walk the streets without disguising my gender and appearance using the Contrarian's Blade of Mirrors so that nobody knew who I was. I wouldn't even have been able to enter the city at all if it wasn't for the small number of allies who still helped me.

On my way here, people I thought were my friends turned on me. The reasons they gave for attacking me were utterly incomprehensible.

The fighter, whose noble character I admired, said I was standing in his way of becoming the ultimate hero.

The dancer, a reassuring sisterly presence, told me she wanted to grant her husband, the fighter, his dream and collect the bounty on my head.

The clumsy wizard, who came to care for me along our quest together, revealed a desire to experiment on me for the purpose of being remembered for generations.

The merchant, who helped me commercialize my modern-day knowledge, tried to kill me out of the fear that I would sell that knowledge to others and threaten his monopoly.

The martial artist, who was unsociable but loved animals, wanted to kill me simply to become stronger.

The assassin, dispatched by the kingdom to assist us and whose information saved our lives on many occasions, told me with cold eyes that the king had ordered my death, and he would not hesitate to obey.

The villagers who helped us on our travels looked at me with greed in their eyes as they admitted they had sold me out for coin.

Finally, there was the kindly priestess, who always cheered everyone up. She declared me the enemy of her God, said I had been corrupted by evil. She never told me the reason for her betrayal.

The kingdom, the empire, the beast lands, the Church. One by one, the lands I'd sworn to protect turned against me. The people believed their leaders without suspicion, and I, whom they had called a hero, became a target of scorn. Even now, I still hadn't come to terms with the fact that I had been betrayed. I wanted to scream at their reasoning. I was reduced to hiding myself like a criminal, my heart burning in a sea of hostility, until at last, I returned to the royal capital. It was tough. It was painful. Many times, I wanted to give up, but the one thing that gave my broken heart solace was the promise I had made to the demon lord.

"Promise me you'll go back to your family. Your home."

…That was what the girl I killed said to me. What a demanding girl she was. Through all the lies, the deceit, the bluff and bluster, behind all the haughty laughter, she was a coward. A crybaby. And she understood me more than anyone else. She brought color into this black-and-white cardboard cutout of a world, and everyone hated her for it.

*   *   *

I clasped the small pouch hanging from my neck. Inside was the magic stone that held the sorceress's evil power. To a demon like her, it was her heart.

It required an enormous amount of mana to summon a hero. The royal family exhausted many of their most precious magical artifacts bringing me over. The sorceress gave me that power in the form of this stone, her own life, all to grant me my wish and let me return to my world.

She said we'd settle things once and for all, with no regrets, and then she let herself get killed.

"It seems I shan't be accompanying you back to your world after all. Well, no matter. You've helped me so much, Kaito. It's about time I gave something back. It's like I said: I never leave a debt unsettled."

"You always did like overkill."

"Promise me you'll go back to your world. Your family. Your home. Oh, but don't forget me too quickly. Be sure to mourn me. Construct a tomb worthy of my greatness and weep as you remember my legacy. Kaito, all you ever think about is your own world. I want to have you to myself for a while! Hee-hee-hee! When I think about it that way, dying doesn't seem so bad after all!"

"Don't give me that. I know you're scared; don't lie to me."

"Oh, and one more thing. Make sure you get all you want out of life. I'm giving you my own, so you had better not waste it. I'll be watching over you, so look out, mister! If I see you slacking off, I'll come back to life and beat you up! Or I'll haunt you!"

"I'd be fine with that, if it meant I got to see you again as a ghost or anything else."

*　　*　　*

Her voice was so burned into my mind, I still heard it when she wasn't around. The last words we shared passed through my thoughts. She was a selfish girl, right to the bitter end, and I was a horrible person for letting her go through with it.

Now that I had slain evil and saved the world, it was my turn to be on the receiving end. She used to call me a fool. Turns out, she was right. I was a fool. An idiot. A coward. I could only regret that I had realized it too late.

"…"

So now I would do anything to keep that promise. I would return home to my family, just as she wanted. It was the only thing keeping me going.

Before I realized it, my tankard was empty.

"Hey there, young lass, sucks to see such a beautiful girl lookin' so down. How 'bout drinks? On us."

"…I'll pass. Barkeep! The money's on the table."

"He…hey! *Tsk…* Not interested, eh?"

After refusing the drunkard's generous invitation, I headed out into the rain, and my hood protected me from the heavy droplets. On rainy nights, the street was bare. I used the effect of the Wing Blade of Detoxification to purge the alcohol from my system before heading to the slums. The people there were grateful to me for saving them when the Wall Eaters destroyed the city barriers and allowed monsters to attack, and they offered me shelter where the kingdom wouldn't find me. I planned to infiltrate the castle the next day and find my way back to the summoning chamber where I had first come to this world. It seemed the king, queen, and knights were all out of the castle at the moment.

I didn't know why the kingdom had betrayed me, or if they truly believed all this talk about me becoming the next demon lord, and although I would have loved to hear the answer, the priority right now was returning to my own world.

"...Looks like I was right to sober up."

I headed down a side road as naturally as possible before turning around and attempting to draw out the people who had been tailing me ever since I left the tavern.

"What do you—? *Ahem*, might you have some business with me? I don't recall doing anything that might capture the attention of two lovely gentlemen such as yourselves."

I suddenly remembered I was supposed to be a woman and corrected my speech. A deathly hush fell over the alley. Just as I thought my pursuers were about to spring a surprise attack, two men dressed in black stepped into view.

"You are the hero, correct? In that case... Urk!"

By combining my mastered Fleet-Foot skill—"Godfoot"—and my mastered Air Step—"Blinkstep"—I teleported behind the two men faster than the eye could see and held my Twin Blades of Shadow to their throats.

"Where did you learn that information? This disguise is too perfect for any of the townsfolk to see through."

"W-wait! The princess sent us! She heard that a woman who looks like the hero was in town and sent us to find her!"

Now that they mentioned it, the two men did look familiar. I recalled seeing them among the princess's entourage.

"Alicia? What does the princess of this traitorous country want with me?"

"Th-the princess herself has not betrayed you! We are your friends! We know what you want, and we braved danger to come find you so that we can return you to your original world, as promised!"

"..."

"The king and queen may have been taken in by the Church's

lies about your succeeding the demon lord and forced you to shoulder all the people's resentment against the kingdom's oppressive rule, but the princess is still on your side! Besides, the summoning ritual is a secret of the royal family, passed down only through oral tradition! You need her help to perform it!"

They had a point. I was not well versed in magic. I couldn't even cast it myself. Either way, I was going to need to learn the ritual from the royal family first. I was planning to do that by searching their library, but if what these men said was true, that would be a fruitless effort since it wasn't written down anywhere.

"...So what do you want with me?" I asked.

"We can take you to the princess right now, if you'd like. Come with us to our hideout. It's okay; we're your *allies*."

...Could I trust them?

I had parted with the princess before my final battle with the demon lord, and I had not seen her since. It was entirely possible what these men said was true, and she was only pretending to go along with her mother and father. If she helped me, I could return to my world immediately. I could put an end to this life on the run. A life spent wading through muddy water.

"*Please just trust us.* The princess has been worried sick about you. That is why she sent us to make contact with you as soon as possible. She said she wanted to help you."

At those words, I choked up. The men before me—they looked like me. Their words were my words. *Please just trust me.* It was all I ever wanted.

"...Okay. I'll come with you."

I removed my blades from their throats, and the two men were visibly relieved.

"Th-thank you. Please follow us. We're heading inside the castle, to the place you first appeared when you were summoned. From there, you'll use a teleportation stone to warp to a safe location while we prepare for the ritual. We don't know who could be watching, so we need to take every precaution, you see."

For purposes of national security, there were small magic items in every town or village that blocked teleportation in or out of the settlement. Otherwise, when war broke out, enemies could bypass the country's defenses. However, there was a location within the castle from which teleportation to any destination was possible. That was the summoning chamber where I had first arrived. Otherwise, it would not have been possible to summon me from my world. The artifacts that suppressed that building's effective range were not buried deep in the ground like the others but were removable to allow for long-distance teleportation.

"All right."

I wanted to say my last good-byes to the people who helped me up to this point, but I decided not to. As long as the world saw me as evil, it would be dangerous for anyone to be affiliated with me. If I could end things without needing to rely on them anymore, then that was best for everyone involved.

Following the black-robed men, I arrived at a small copse on the outskirts of the city.

"Hey, I thought we were going to the castle," I called out.

"Indeed. There's a path within this forest that leads straight to the summoning chamber within the palace."

I walked with the two men deeper into the forest, and before long, they began to rummage around on the ground, searching for something. Within about ten seconds, they found what they were looking for and lifted up a huge square-shaped slab of rock. Heading down into the hole, I was greeted by a thick carpet of dust and a scent of damp and mold that I was well used to by now. The stone staircase and stale air were certainly in line with what I expected a secret underground passage to be like.

"This way, please. If you could watch your step."

The two men retrieved candles from their pockets to light the way, and we descended into the passage. The tunnel remained level for a while, the air heavy and stagnant, and for the longest time, the only sound was the echo of our footsteps on the flagstones.

Then at last, we reached a dead end, and when the two men lifted the ceiling, I found myself once more in the familiar summoning chamber from all those years ago.

"Ah, Hero! I'm so glad to see that you made it!"

I looked to the source of the voice, and standing right there, smiling like a flower, was Princess Alicia, looking as beautiful and delicate as the day I met her. She had been fifteen then, and while she had certainly grown up magnificently in the subsequent years, she had not changed at all in some ways.

"Are you hurt, Hero?"

"O-oh, no, Princess. I'm surprised you knew—"

"—That it was you? You have told me about the Contrarian's Blade of Mirrors before."

The princess broke into a familiar smile. Seeing it put my mind at ease. It was like nothing had happened, like we were still back before things went so wrong. I had decided to trust her—that was why I was here—but part of me had still feared she would turn on me like all the others, attacking me with her signature Light magic as soon as she saw me.

"I'm sure you have many questions, but we have no time. Take this teleportation stone and activate it by charging it with mana. It should work so long as you're in this room."

The princess handed me a semitransparent yellow crystal. It was an item I had used many times before.

"Once you arrive, we can talk further. I'll teach you the ritual to return to your world there."

"Okay. Thank you."

I channeled my mana into the teleportation stone, and it began to glow. The spell encoded within the stone activated, and a magic circle spread out and encompassed me.

At that moment, the princess laughed.

"Hee-hee. Oh, what a hopeless fool you are."

Before I could respond to her mocking words, I was shrouded in light and whisked off. The last thing I saw was the princess's true face as the veneer of respectability peeled away.

As soon as the teleportation ended, I immediately sensed danger and channeled mana into my emergency soul blade, the Aegis Blade of Shielding. A split second later, an unimaginable barrage of spells rained down on me. Through my enhanced Reaction Time, I could see each and every one of them in detail. A blazing fireball. A razor-sharp icicle. An invisible blade of wind. A boulder heavy enough to crush me. A spear of pure light. A grasping shadow. Over a hundred different spells descended upon me, seeking my death, and this magic... I'd felt it somewhere before.

I dispelled my disguise and prepared for battle. When the dust and rubble that had been thrown into the air by the attack settled, I saw hundreds upon hundreds of knights, the scars across their faces a testament to their combat experience. Leading them was the man who taught me how to fight, the royal-knight commander, and beside him, her long silver hair still glowing with the mana from her spells, was Princess Alicia.

"Honestly, for being such an idiot, you're as stubborn as a mule."

I quickly assessed my surroundings. I was in some sort of arena beneath a vast dome, and I recognized it as the Guardian Room of a dungeon we had encountered along our quest, the Fuuga Ruins. Given that I would expect the Guardian to have revived by now, they must have defeated it again, and indeed, I could see that the Dungeon Core behind the princess had lost its magical glow. It would have been easy enough for them to do if they knew how to take it down. After all, it was with these knights' help that I had defeated the boss in the first place.

"...Alicia. So you've betrayed me, too?!"

"Betrayed you? Oh my, no. To do that, I would have to be your ally first, no? It's not a betrayal if I was never on your side to begin with. Could you imagine? A princess teaming up with a filthy other-worlder? Just the thought of it makes my skin crawl. Thank heavens I don't have to put on that disgusting act any longer."

She smiled. It was her true nature, unclouded by deceit.

"Honestly, if you'd just crawl over and die already, I could wash my hands of all this. You're like a gutter rat. Oh well, I suppose it'll be over soon enough."

"Alicia...you...!"

"You can't teleport out of here, can you? And we're far from any city, so we don't have to worry about causing damage. We control the exits, and you're far outnumbered. Even you won't last long."

She was telling the truth. It was impossible to *activate* teleportation magic while in a Guardian Room. You could teleport in, but not out. My only hope would be to get out of this room to somewhere I could teleport from, but it wasn't possible for me to fight my way through hundreds of the kingdom's best warriors to the room's sole exit. Maybe I stood a chance if some of them were the inexperienced rank and file, but that wasn't the case here. There was no way for me to break through.

"I must say I'm glad you're so stupid. You were so easy to trick. Even those commoners living near the slums deceived you."

"Wh-what? ...No!"

"Indeed. Ever since you arrived in the city, they've been reporting your movements to me. All I needed to do was drop them a couple of gold coins and they told me *everything*."

"...Krh..."

"Now it's our turn to help you."

"Of course we'd pay back our debt!"

The images of the villagers who'd helped me flashed through my mind. They had gone against me, too.

"...Dammit! How could they stab me in the back so easily?!"

I felt anger at being betrayed and disappointment in myself.

Why hadn't I been more distrustful? I had been in the city for only two days, and people came in and out of it all the time. How would anyone have noticed that there was a woman in town who looked like the hero when I wasn't even showing my face?

And what about this supposed hideout? Why hadn't I realized it before? The summoning chamber may let you teleport to any location, but that didn't apply in reverse. If this safe house was outside the city, how was I supposed to teleport back in?

I was naive. I had failed to notice what was going on. I could console myself by saying I had been tired from my long journey, from my life as a fugitive, but it was cold comfort now.

"Why...? Why would you go so far just to kill me?!"

"Oh my, stalling for time? Fine by me. I suppose you have done rather well for a rat. Very well, I shall entertain you."

The princess chuckled, giving me a scornful look the likes of which I had never seen.

I would never die before fulfilling my promise and returning to my world. I needed something, anything, to get myself out of this situation. My darting eyes fell at last upon Princess Alicia herself.

...Everything I had seen in her until now had been an act.

"It's not good for the royal family to have someone running about with so much power. As long as you live, it threatens the peace and stability of our nation. The seeds of rebellion are sprouting. Therefore, we must have you take all our citizens' discontent. Then by killing you, we can crush that potential unrest as well."

"I can't believe you…"

"Or at least, that's what Mother and Father would say, but the true reason is that I simply cannot permit you to exist. Oh, how revolting it is that an otherworlder like you is allowed to wear our beautiful skin, speak our beautiful words, and live in our beautiful world! I thought demihumans and beastfolk were repulsive enough, but you're even more sickening than them! It's foul! Do you have any idea how hard it was for me to hold back my vomit while we traveled together?"

"…Gh!"

She wasn't just treating me with contempt. In her eyes, I wasn't a human at all. She looked at me like I was a piece of filth rotting before her. Like my mere existence offended her to her very core.

But then her face changed in an instant, back to the smiling flower I had seen *so many times before.*

"However, I will do one last thing for you," she stated. "I'll teach you how to get back to your own world, like I promised I would."

Alicia laughed, as if she found the idea funny. As put off as I was by her sudden transformation, I felt something else. Something deeply disturbing.

"No lies, I promise. To prove it, I'll even swear using the Oath of Fidelity."

The "Oath of Fidelity" was a means for users of spirit magic to verify their claims. If they swore falsely by it, the caster would lose whatever they specified in the oath, along with the ability to ever cast spirit magic again.

"I swear, in the presence of the myriad spirits, that my words on the summoning ritual and ritual of departure be true, and may the spirits take my arm if not. *Oath of Fidelity.*"

Alicia's body was enveloped in a pale light, indicating that the spell was successful. As long as the light surrounded her, Alicia could not tell a lie or else she would lose her arm.

"Now, I shall reveal all."

Alicia smiled a sadistic smile, one she could never show as a princess. The mere sight of her set alarm bells ringing in my mind.

Why was she going to so much trouble to make it clear she wasn't lying?

Why would she tell me what I wanted to know right before she killed me?

Alicia's motives worried me, but I recognized this as an opportunity. I needed to find a way out of here, but I was also desperately in need of the ritual to take me home. Under this oath, it was basically impossible for her to lie.

"The ritual itself is simple. Like other rituals, all you need to perform it is the appropriate tribute. For the hero summoning and sending ritual, you need an item containing an enormous amount of mana, the ancient inscriptions found in the summoning chamber, and one other thing. What do you suppose that is?"

"One other thing, huh...?"

Summoning me required the royal family to give up several of their most powerful artifacts. The more you had, the less powerful the individual tributes needed to be, but in order to count as tributes, these objects had to be above a certain power level. Higher-quality items could hold more mana. For weapons and armor, that meant the materials it was made of, how it was constructed, and the skill of the person who created it. It was incredibly hard to find items of high enough quality to use as ritual tributes, not to mention the vast reserves of mana you had to imbue them with. Even a kingdom would struggle to locate such items. That was why I held on so tightly to that bag around my neck.

"There's something else you need...?!"

"Indeed. No amount of mana alone is enough to defy heaven's rule, even for an instant. Did you never consider that?"

Alicia flashed me an innocent smile. Then as if to deny me the thought, she spoke in a voice laced with venom.

"There are four steps to the ritual. The first is to open a portal in the space-time of this world. Next, you must open a portal in the space-time of the other world. Then you must create a path that bridges the two portals. Finally, you must draw the summoning target through. Each of these steps requires one tribute, and the mana is just for priming the ritual and drawing the target out. So what do you suppose the other tributes are?"

"..."

I understood very little in the ways of ritual magic. The only ritual I knew offered a few medicinal herbs as tribute to apply a detoxifying effect. I had seen larger rituals performed, but I didn't know what the tributes were. This type of magic was already arcane enough.

"Tee-hee. Very well. Then I shall give you a hint. In order to complete the first step..."

A chill of fear ran up my spine.

"...in the place in which the portal was to be opened..."

Don't listen, my body was saying. I wanted to plug my ears and drown out her voice. But I had to listen. I needed to hear what she would say. I had to know.

"...two hundred members of the humanoid race were put to death."

I felt the blood drain from my face. Pleased by my reaction, Alicia had on a demonic smile.

"Hee-hee-hee. Allow me to ask you a different question. On our side, we used beastfolk slaves captured from abroad. Now...

* * *

"…what do you suppose we used for the bridge and the other portal?"

Wh-what the hell…?

If opening a portal on this side required a sacrifice of two hundred of this world's people…

…then surely, to open a portal in my world, it would need… But that would mean…

"Now, tell me, Hero. Didn't you mention to me before where you were and who you were with when you were summoned? Why don't you tell me what was used for the portal first?"

I had been in my classroom at school. Then the offering would have been the people there with me…

…which would have been my teachers and friends?

"You're…you're lying."

"I'm not. It's the truth. Look, my arms are still here. The people who died when you were summoned were the two hundred people physically closest to you at the time."

Somewhere deep inside me, I heard my heart crack.

"You little shiiiiits!"

""""""*Restraining Thorns!*""""""

"Gah! Grh!"

Fueled by anger, I summoned my most powerful soul blade. However, before I could take a single step, magical chains appeared to hold me back. The chains, covered in gray spikes, obeyed the wills of the magical knights who summoned them, rising up out of the ground and trapping me like a net. I was unharmed thanks to the Clothes of Dark Spirits I wore, but the bindings left me unable to move in the slightest.

"Tee-hee! Like I said, it's the truth."

"Shut it! I'll murder you! Get the hell out of my way, dammit!"

I was seething, seized by an uncontrollable rage. I struggled against my chains, but all I could do was rattle them powerlessly. Alicia watched me with the biggest grin on her face.

"…Now, that just leaves the question of the bridge, doesn't it?"

It was like an ice cube had been slipped down my back.

"Wait… What do you mean…? You mean…there's more…?"

The dread was clear in my voice as my lips faltered while trying to put together the words.

What more was she going to say? What other terrors did that monstrous smile have to reveal?

"The space between worlds is the divine realm. No human can survive such a transgression unaided."

I didn't want to listen. I didn't want to listen. I didn't want to listen. What else did she sacrifice to bring me over here?

"It's said that those who intrude upon the divine realm are marked with great power. That is why heroes arrive in this world with powerful intrinsic abilities. However, that is of little use to us if the hero is dead on arrival. Thus, a bridge is required that allows the hero to pass from one world to the other safely, while still receiving the power of the divine."

My friends. My teachers. Two hundred people. What was left for them to take?

Then Alicia said her final words, drenched in pleasure, as if she were biting into the tender flesh of a cherry and tasting its sweet juices.

"The materials required, the tribute for that step, are five people whose souls are aligned with your own. For example…

"........your parents, your siblings, your grandparents. Your relatives."

I heard a sound, like my world was being pinched out by the princess's poison-stained fingers.

"What...are you saying? Huh...? No...that's not... I mean..."

My mouth was forming words, but I had already stopped thinking. I had no idea what I was saying.

"I'm saying they're dead! Your family, your friends. They all died so you could come here!"

They're dead? Mom? Dad? Mai? Suehiko? Kenta? Yuuto? Mr. Oogane?

Why? Why? Why? Why, why, why, why? That means I can't go back! I promised her. I promised I'd go back and see my family. I told her. I'd go back. I promised. AAAAAAAAAAAAAAAAAHHH!

"Ah-ha-ha-ha-ha-ha! Look at your face! That's what I wanted to see! Ah-ha-ha! Hey, how does it feel? You wanted to go back to your world, didn't you? See your family? Your friends? Well, they've been dead this whole time, you little shit! Ha-ha-ha-ha!"

Her shrill laughter was like a blade between my ribs. I could feel myself falling apart.

"You won't believe how hard I had to try not to laugh when you first told me! That was the only time I found it tolerable to be with you, because you were so damn funny!"

My world spun. Forward, backward, right, left, up, down, it all blended together into one big, oversaturated blur.

"Stop... Just... Please stop..."

" 'I'd like to go back home. Mess around with my friends again. Eat dinner with my family again.' That's what you sounded like before you went off to kill that dumb shrew. Well? I thought that was a pretty darn good impression of you."

This was it. I was breaking down.

The sound of creaking branches, of cracking glass. My world was being replaced with something else.

"Still want to go back? Go right ahead. Rape some beastfolk girls, make some little half-breed babies, and they should be enough to get you a bridge back! Actually, don't do that, or I'll have to kill them. I don't want otherworlder spawn spreading its filth in this world even for a second."

"Ngh!! Aliciaaaaaaaaaaaaa!"

My mana rushed into my arms and legs, fueled by my rage, and I tore apart the chains that bound me.

"Now! Concentrate fire!" ordered the knight commander.

"Grrraaarghhh! Get out of my way!" I screamed. The knights fired their spells at me, but I didn't even look in their direction.

I was burned with fire, shot with water, sliced by wind, beaten with stone, pierced with light, and tormented by darkness, and yet the one thing that drove me was the thought of using the sword in my hand to stab Princess Alicia right through her rotten heart. Any desire to get away had long since disappeared. As the soldiers brandished their weapons, I dashed between them to arrive before her.

"Diiiiiiie!"

I swung my sword toward her with all my rage.

"Grh! Grrrgaaah!"

"Tee-hee. What a fool you are. Couldn't even see through that illusion? How pathetic."

Her body had dissolved into a fine mist, and dozens of arrows landed in my back.

My Clothes of Dark Spirits had exhausted all their power getting me through the barrage of spells and could not stop the ensuing onslaught.

"Now, I'm afraid the show is over. As thanks for entertaining me, I shall end your life personally. What an honor. You, hand me your sword."

A knight standing near the princess produced his weapon, and Alicia took it in her hands before slowly walking toward me.

"Hey, Kaito."

In my last moments, I heard the voice of the girl they called evil.

"I'll do anything and everything I can for you. I'll give you half the world if I must. So please come to my side."

I wasn't able to hold her trembling hand.

She knew I would refuse. She knew I wouldn't take it.

She was left to cry her cold tears alone.

It was my fault. I made a mistake. I was wrong.

And this was my punishment. I was finally going to pay the price for my stupidity.

"Promise me you'll go back to your world." The life she had given for me, the promise we had made. It was all for nothing. My home had already been taken away from me for good.

"Now die, you monster from another world wearing our skin."

I was about to be killed, but my mind was flooded with regret.

"Make sure you get all you want out of life. I'm giving you my own, so you had better not waste it. I'll be watching over you, so look out, mister!"

The moment the princess's sword plunged toward my heart, I remembered those words.

"Wh-what is the meaning of this?!"

Alicia's sword never reached my chest. There was a ringing sound

as it struck the *demon heart* hanging around my neck. The accumulated power of the demon lord flowed out of it and flooded into the Guardian Core. It was enough to revive the Guardian immediately.

""Graaaaaargh!""

There was a sharp, screeching roar as two beasts appeared. A lion and a tiger, clad in red and blue flames respectively.

"A-all units, prepare for battle! Protect the princess!"

The knights scrambled to react to this unexpected foe.

...Now was my only chance to escape.

"Raaaargh!"

"What?! Dammit! The hero's getting away!"

I didn't try anything fancy; I just ran for the door, forcing my way through the line of soldiers while they were distracted by the Guardian's appearance. Applying Blinkstep and Godfoot to build up speed, I activated Air Step to leap into the air, using as little movement as possible to dodge any incoming attacks—otherwise, I'd just let them hit me and stifle my screams of pain as best I could. All I cared about was reaching the exit.

"Stop! Don't let him escape! If he takes even one step out of here..."

I heard the princess's voice from behind me and gripped my soul blade tighter. Even if it meant my certain death, I could go back right now and make sure she died...

"I'm giving you my own, so you had better not waste it."

"Goddamn! Scatter! *Blade of Misery: Scarlet Thunder!*" I shouted.

"Raise your shields!" roared the knight commander.

Then our voices were drowned out by a peal of thunder and an explosion that crackled with lightning. Of course, I wasn't expecting to deal serious damage, but I forced them to stop for a second and throw up their shields and magical barriers, and the knights farther back were too busy fighting the Guardian to come after me.

"Stop right there!"

"Gaaagh!"

A firebolt from the princess scorched my back, but it was too late.

"Come ba—"

The princess's words were cut off as I activated my soul blade and teleported away. The last thing I saw as I looked behind me was her face, twisted beyond all recognition with indignant rage.

I wished to be anywhere else, as far away as possible. When I opened my eyes, I was in a strange forest I had not seen before. The trees reached up around me, obscuring the moon and the clouds from view and leaving me standing in a profound darkness as the rainwater drizzled down my body and caused my wounds to sting.

My back burned with pain from the princess's spell, but as soon as I thought about healing it, my mind spun. Long-distance teleportation required an enormous amount of mana. I had almost forgotten the feeling of mana withdrawal. It seemed I wouldn't be able to heal my injuries just yet.

Pulling an arrow out of myself and applying pressure to the wound, I tried to walk but found myself unable to take even a single step.

"..."

The people I wanted to help. The people I trusted. They'd been my enemies all along.

I'd always thought that someday, I would go home—that someday, my life would return to normal. That thought kept me going through all the hard times, but it, too, was a lie. Nothing but a mirage on the horizon that vanished when I got close. What was I supposed to do now? Why was I still alive?

"Ha-ha… What the…?"

I smiled in self-pity. I didn't know the answers.

"Make sure you get all you want out of life."

I took a step, even as I felt like my legs were about to give up. I knew not what for, but I wasn't going to die.

It was because of her that I had grown to like this world.

It was because of her that I learned to smile in this world.

She told me I wasn't allowed to waste my life.

And I knew that if I died, she would simply call me a fool, and a coward, and laugh the way she always did, but that wasn't the point. It was for my own sake that I couldn't afford to stop here.

If I went back on my word and ended it all now, I could never stand by her side, even in death.

I had to keep walking.

I hoped my tears, at least, could be forgiven.

"I'm sorry, Leticia. I can't keep my promise. I'm sorry. I'm so sorry…"

My words were snatched up by darkness and stolen by the night.

EPILOGUE
The Hero Laughs While Walking the Path of Vengeance a Second Time

I was floating through a murky sea.

The dream had ended. I was drifting between wakefulness and sleep. Below me stretched the infinite depths. Above me, I could see the bright surface of the water.

"Kaito..."

Suddenly, a wavering shadow appeared before me, and I heard a voice as if from far away, strained through the abyss.

"Leticia..."

Her hair, a deep scarlet, redder than blood. Her gleaming black eyes. Her small, childlike body. Her dress, as black as night. She looked exactly as I last saw her. She was Leticia Lu Harleston, the forty-seventh demon lord.

"Kaito... Come to me..."

"Come on, brain! Are you really going to make her say that?!" I said out loud.

I couldn't help but laugh at myself. I knew just how pathetic I was, crying out over a dream that had reminded me of the past. How dependent was I on the girl I had killed with my own hands?

"But I suppose you're right. I will get to see you again."

And I would.

The Leticia who was still alive knew nothing about me. It would be nothing but sentimentality. Nothing more than selfish closure and atonement. Still, I longed to see her just one more time. Just to say one thing to her, and she'd never have to see me again.

I wanted to apologize. I wanted to wish her well and say good-bye.

"And when I do, I'm going to say, *O Lord, please take revenge with me, and I shall grant you half the world.*"

She wouldn't know what I was taking revenge for, and I would not tell her. It was for me to deal with. Therefore, this was a request she could never accept. It would be my punishment for the sin of being the only one to know what those words meant.

I knew she wouldn't understand. I knew she would refuse me. But I had to tell her. I had to.

… Then perhaps at last, I can let you go. Perhaps I can live, even without you by my side.

Ah, but…

"It's such a shame I won't be able to be by your side when I'm dead."

"…ster……aster…"

"Ngh… Ah… Minnalis?"

I was gently shaken awake to see Minnalis's face centimeters from my own, her cheeks slightly reddened.

I knew I had been sleeping, but I remembered falling asleep with my back to the wall and one knee in my arms. Now I was lying on my back, and I could feel something dangerously soft behind my head.

"Good morning, Master. You were talking in your sleep."

"Hmm? Oh, I was dreaming of the past… Wait, what is this?"

"Oh, the Guardian Room was bigger than I expected. I had to use all my MP on Intoxicating Phantasm, and I'm feeling a little tipsy…"

I'd also fallen asleep from mana withdrawal, so I guess she couldn't resist, but even when it would be easy for her to get carried away, Minnalis did the responsible thing. She seemed embarrassed to have me in her lap, though—her usual poker face was failing her, and her lips were starting to tremble.

...Would it be bad to tease her a bit? Would that make me a terrible person? Her face was begging to be bullied, but I summoned up every bit of my adult self-restraint and refrained.

MP drunkenness is no joke. Regular drunkenness is no joke, either. Taking advantage of a drunk person is a despicable act. Besides, you never know when you'll be the one in that position.

I stood up and shook my head, as if to dispel the remains of my drowsiness and tipsiness.

"How long was I asleep?" I asked.

"About an hour, I would say."

"I see. And is the Guardian dead?"

"I don't think so. Our experience hasn't gone up."

The hole I had made in the door was now plugged with scraps of garm fur. I could hear noises of the Guardian struggling in pain on the other side, so the poison appeared to be working as intended.

This plan was not perfect. It required that you punch a hole in the near-indestructible Guardian Door, and on top of that, you needed a poison strong enough to damage the Guardian itself. Guardians were incredibly resistant to status conditions, and this dungeon's boss, the Goblin King, was no exception. What's more, if the poison was strong enough, then it would even damage the weapons, armor, and materials that the Guardian dropped. To counteract that, you would have to rush into the poison-filled room as soon as the Guardian fell. (If you left them, the drops would eventually be absorbed back into the dungeon along with the Guardian's body.)

The only reason we could use this plan was because we had the unnatural powers of the Pyrachnid's Claw and the everlasting poison of Minnalis's Intoxicating Phantasm, coupled with the fact that all we cared about were the experience points.

Another concern was that I wanted to keep my soul blades and their powers secret, but there was nobody around to see them this time, so we didn't need to worry about that.

"Well, while we're waiting for the Guardian to die, I'll allocate my experience."

I wasn't going to get any experience points from the boss, because it was Minnalis who was doing all the damage. That meant I already had everything I was going to get from this dungeon.

Right now, I had around fifteen thousand EXP left. I'd spent three thousand on the Squirrel's Blade of Holding, four thousand on the Fairy's Blade of Water, and thirty-six thousand on the Wing Blade of Detoxification. That came to a little under sixty thousand EXP that I'd gained in this dungeon. If I wasn't in debt and I put it all into leveling, that would be enough to get me past level 50.

Unlocking the Fairy's Blade and the Wing Blade taught me something else. I could unlock the sealed abilities of my soul blades incrementally. The Fairy's Blade had an ability that let you control the temperature of the water it produced, while the Wing Blade had abilities for resisting and curing all the various status conditions. However, each of these abilities required experience points to unlock.

I spent six thousand to unlock the blade itself, two thousand for each resistance (Poison, Paralysis, Sleep, Petrification, and Charm), and then twenty thousand to let me extend those effects to my allies. That made thirty-six thousand in total. This last ability could be upgraded to allow for a maximum of ten people to share the status-resistance effects, but for now, I could use it on just three people. That shouldn't be too much of a problem since I wasn't planning on surrounding myself with a bunch of random hangers-on like the last time.

Anyway, back to how to distribute my remaining fifteen thousand. I considered putting it toward my debt, but if I was increasing my stats, it was going to be harder to gain more experience in the future. It would be better to spend those experience points on a soul blade that I could use to counteract that effect.

To put it in video-game terms, the first time around was a normal playthrough. This time, I was playing with restrictions. That meant I had a few options available to me.

Challenger's Blade of Adversity

This sword grew in power the lower my stats were compared with my opponent's. If my stats were higher, the sword would get weaker instead.

Attacker's Needle of Poison

This sword strengthened the effect of Poison on the target every time it dealt a hit, regardless of the damage caused. However, I couldn't apply Poison to the sword itself, so I would need Minnalis's help to make good use of it.

Boundary Blade

For a bit of mana, this blade could produce a barrier that reflected ranged attacks back toward the attacker. The sword's own attack power was practically nonexistent, however, so I wouldn't be able to defeat an enemy any other way with it.

Considering my current stats and MP, it was going to have to be one of these three. As I was thinking things over, a bright flash of light suddenly emanated out of my pocket.

"Master?!"

"Ah, don't worry, it's okay."

I reached inside and pulled out a small glass bottle. It was the one Jufain had given to me in the slums. I opened it and placed it on the ground, whereupon the golden liquid inside began to move around like a slime. It crawled out of the bottle and toward the nearby wall.

"That took longer than I thought. There's no point if the princess's burns have already healed by now. Let's take a look and see…"

I had gone to great pains to disguise this magic so that it wouldn't be discovered before I could see the beautiful sight it was going to reveal to me. I mean, it was only going to be more torment like I inflicted on her at the start, but there was no such thing as overkill in this business. It's just a pity that all I could do was confirm if my plan had gone off. I had wanted to watch the princess suffer.

While I was thinking, the slime climbed up onto the wall before stopping at about chest height. There, it flattened out and expanded into the rough shape of a TV monitor. On its body, an image formed of someplace far away…

"What's that…?" asked Minnalis.

"It's the royal throne room. You saw it in my vision, didn't you?"

There in the image were the king and queen, the knights, and Princess Alicia.

It had been over ten days since that perfidious wretch betrayed me.

That day, I performed the hero summoning, just as the Great Spirits commanded. I gathered the required sacrifices, and the ritual had been a success.

However, the hero I had summoned was unruly, if not insane.

And to think that just once, I was willing to allow a worm to dream of becoming a hero.

"...Krh."

The scars on my back burned.

I will not follow your orders.
Let the scum I send you be a warning.
Your punishment will be many times more painful.
Prepare to lose all you hold dear.

                                                         The Revenant

My attendants said my skin was lovely as porcelain. Now it was ravaged by scars. Recovery magic could restore HP, but wounds like this would heal only with time. Only someone on the level of the archbishop of the Church could cast a spell strong enough to heal them completely.

Still, I had been having healing spells cast on me day after day, and the scars were fading. A few more days, and the message would be gone completely. I was no longer in any pain, but every time I remembered that man's face, I felt a festering urge inside me.

On that day, soon after he left the room, I blacked out, as if fleeing from the unbearable pain. It was only the following day that I was rescued by the knights waiting outside, and when I next awoke, I was in my bedchamber within the castle.

The most powerful knights, including the knight commander, were covered in the scars of their many battles. They left them that way on purpose to strike fear into their enemies on the battlefield, but needless to say, it made them look quite vicious. For that reason, I had brought only my most noble-looking knights into the summoning chamber, so as to not scare the fledgling hero. Now half of them were still recovering in the infirmary.

Even with all medical resources diverted to myself, it was only a whole day after I was rescued that my burned throat was cured and I was first able to speak.

When they found us, the knights were a wretched sight, their arms and legs bent out of shape and broken, their faces beaten to a bloody pulp. It was a wonder that some of them were still alive. I lay there, my face bruised and my disheveled hair sprawling across the floor, with that hateful message scorched into my back.

It was impossible to tell at a glance what had happened, but it was clearly no accident. However, there was no information about the perpetrator to go on. The building had been surrounded by knights, so at first, it appeared as though he had simply teleported far away to safety. It was only when I could finally explain what had happened that searches were carried out in the capital.

The necklace he stole…for *"a bit of spending money,"* he had said. That treasure proved I was next in line to the throne. He couldn't simply sell it at a shop, because it was inscribed with the royal crest. Even if he tried to take it elsewhere, out of the capital, word would get around.

That necklace was passed down to me by my late sister. It wasn't for a beast like that to handle… No—it wasn't for anyone but me to touch!

"You'll pay for this…"

He would pay. The necklace would be returned to me, and that man would suffer for what he did. I would make him beg for mercy at my feet. Then he would be put to death.

However, although my knights had spent the last few days investigating, they hadn't turned up any strong leads. It was possible he'd already fled the capital by now.

The day prior, one noble claimed to have found the necklace. This man was a count who was considered something of a nuisance by the people of the city, owing largely to his strong regard for the law and his overinquisitive nature. Supposedly, the necklace had turned up in a shipment of contraband that he had confiscated, and he was going to present it in the royal court today.

"Princess, it's time," said a handmaiden.

"Yes, I know," I replied.

I checked my attire one last time, then headed to the throne room.

Atop his throne sat my father, King Rogia Orollea, a sturdily built man. Beside him was my mother, past forty but no less beautiful than she was in her youth, Queen Lecilia Orollea. And on his other side was where I sat. Also nearby was the prime minister, Roebentz, and Guidott, the knight commander, who stood close at hand, ready to leap to my defense if anyone were to threaten me.

"I would hereby like to return this item to the care of the royal family."

The young count kneeled before us, and a handmaiden carefully took the necklace along with the pedestal atop which it sat and brought them over to me. As much as I wanted to rush out of my seat and snatch it back, I waited patiently for the handmaiden to get here before taking the necklace and placing it around my neck.

Immediately, I felt the mana running through it. Then the necklace glowed briefly with a pale-green light before returning to normal.

"■■■■■■! Are ■■■ okay?"

My father turned to me and asked me a question, but I didn't hear some of what he said.

"Yes, Father. I'm fine."

I gave myself a quick look-over but could detect nothing out of the ordinary.

"■ see. But then what was that light? ...■■■■■■■■, ■■■■■■■, do ■■■ two know anything?"

"■■■■, ■ am but a mere knight. Perhaps the ■■■■■ ■■■■■■■ can tell ■■ more?"

"Wait, it couldn't be...," the prime minister muttered with a serious look on his face.

However, by this point, I had already figured out what had happened to me.

"■■ ■■■■■, ■ am not a specialist in these matters so ■ cannot be certain, but that light... Perhaps ■■ are dealing with a curse of some description."

"By the heavens... Surely not. The ■ ■ ■ ■ ■ ■ ■ appears to be well."

"F-Father...I cannot hear you. No, to be precise...I cannot hear any words that refer to people."

"Wh-what?! What is the meaning of this?"

I could hear most of what the others said, but names and pronouns failed to reach my ears. I hurried to remove the necklace.

"I... I can't take it off! It won't come off!"

The mention of a curse sent me into a panic. I didn't fully understand what was happening. The next few hours were a jumbled blur. First, we gathered together everyone in the court who was familiar with magic. However, they were mostly trained in combat magic and had little knowledge of the theory underlying it. All we could discover was that a priest would not suffice to dispel this magic. It seemed further investigation was required into the nature of the curse, and the high level of disguise that had been placed on it necessitated someone with specialized knowledge. Researchers were called in from the nearby academy town, and a few days later, they set about experimenting on the artifact.

"That is enough for today. Please leave me. I wish to be alone."

The researchers departed, and I was left to grind my teeth in frustration. Around this time of year, I would normally be networking and strengthening my *connections*. This kingdom was founded by a woman, and female rulers were taken no less seriously than male ones. Nonetheless, I still needed to show my face in order to be respected as the next queen, and so it was important for me to mingle with high society. However, as I was now, I couldn't hear people's names, or even words like *he*, *she*, *I*, *you*, or *them*. It was little impediment when talking to people I didn't know, but it was critical if I was to make a splash in the court scene.

Though the academy had sent its finest researchers, I was told it would take two months at minimum to get to the bottom of this enigma. Even in the best-case scenario, there was no telling what effect two months of reclusion would have on my social standing.

"*Sigh*, it's no use. I'm getting myself into a rut again."

I was getting tired. I drank a cup of warm milk and got out of my chair, adjusting the hem of my nightie. Then I got into my bed, which was stuffed with the finest monster fur, and fell asleep almost instantly.

...I didn't know that my sleepless nights were about to begin.

"Aaaaaaargh!"

"Krh, it's no use! My healing magic is having no effect!"

"Dammit. Why aren't the academy researchers here yet?"

It was the middle of the night, and my father had hurriedly called a nurse to my bedroom. It had been three days since I first put on the necklace, and the true nature of its curse was making itself clear. The scars on my back, which had been recovering, were now growing worse and worse with each passing day. Almost as if the healing *was being undone*. I was racked with scorching pain, as though my burns were still fresh.

"Grrrggghhh! Haaah, haaarghhh!"

It reached the point where I could no longer bear to lie on my back. It felt like each cut was being gouged out anew with a needle. I knew this was the necklace's doing because of the pale light that shrouded my wounds every time the pain flared up, but that information did nothing to help against the pain, nor did any of the healing magic we had access to.

The pain was warping my perception of time. At some point, Father and the nurse had left my room. Or had I asked them to leave? It was shameful as a princess for them to see me this way.

"You'll pay for this..."

I had no proof, but I just knew that he was behind all this. So I could bear the pain. I didn't need any help. All I needed to do was capture the dark feelings that the pain induced. Wrap them in charred-black chains and pull them down deeper and deeper into the tar pit within my heart.

For defiling my family treasure, I would drive that otherworlder, that monster in human skin, to the depths of despair.

"You'll pay... You'll pay... I will have my revenge!"

I reveled in that night as jet-black hate stewed inside me. I didn't let one second of it go to waste.

"Grrr! Graaaargh! Hrgh! Hhh! Aaaaaargh!"

And so the night passed without me ever knowing the peace of sleep.

"All righty. Looked like it went off without a hitch."

Seeing the princess enveloped in glowing light was proof that my machinations had succeeded. She had figured out the first effect, my modified "Impair Senses" that made her unable to hear names and pronouns, and the scene had been exceedingly fun to watch.

The necklace originally came with four effects: Auto HP Regen, Recovery Boost, Record Illusion, and Self-Damage Repair (Poor). I had modified two of these, removed one, and added an extra one in its place.

First was Record Illusion. I had changed this one into Impair Senses.

Then I converted Auto HP Regen into "Reverse Healing (Extra Poor)." This effect healed wounds by "rewinding" the wound until

it was completely gone. This meant that if it was activated when the wound was in the midst of healing, it would rewind that healing back to the wound's worst state and then heal from there.

However, that would all go to waste if she took the necklace off, so I removed the third effect, Recovery Boost, and replaced it with "Prevent Removal." Then I disguised the changes so that only a well-trained professional with an astute eye would notice the difference.

It was the Tailor's Hook of Mending that allowed me to rewrite the effects of magic items. However, it was not omnipotent and required an enormous amount of MP. Just altering effects into similar ones was bad enough, but completely deleting them and replacing them with different ones was effectively impossible without some way of restoring your MP. It worked off a percentage of your max MP, so I could at least accomplish this despite my low level, but that also meant that I couldn't avoid experiencing mana withdrawal, even at higher levels.

The process itself was very difficult and required the full extent of my Finesse and Reaction Time stats. It was also impossible to decrease the time it took to complete. In addition, you couldn't make a magic item more powerful by modifying its effects. The overall power level of the artifact had to be lower than what it was before. That meant I couldn't keep adding more and more harmful effects to the necklace.

"*Pfft!* Look at her face! And she thought she was so cool just a moment ago! Aw, man, definitely worth sixty gold for sure!"

"I didn't think simply watching her reaction would be so enjoyable… Oh, can we change the angle? That pillar is getting in the way."

We spent some time just watching the screen and laughing at the hardship that had befallen everyone in the palace.

"Oh, I think the Guardian's dead," observed Minnalis soon after the video ended.

She cleared her poison out of the room, and we went inside to find the Goblin King's corroded body along with all his equipment.

"Let's grab the Core and get out of here," I said. "The monsters in the forest outside will respawn soon, and the Poison Garm will recruit them into its herd. If we go back now, we might get to see some of the townsfolk or the soldiers getting captured by monsters and taken into the forest. Wouldn't want to miss that!"

"Quite right, Master. We can collect ingredients for tea while listening to the beautiful screams of the worms who betrayed you!"

The garm packs could not stray far from the depths of the forest, so chances were that even if they got into the capital, they would take their prey back to the forest to eat it. Of course, a soldier could easily deal with a single garm, but the pack that would attack the capital would be led by a variant Poison Garm. Last time, there were about forty-four monsters in all.

But the Poison Garm was smart. It had been watching me ever since I entered the forest, and it had seen that I could fight monsters effectively. This time, it would come prepared with a much larger pack, and perhaps there would even be multiple Poison Garm, too.

I couldn't wait to see those worms become wolf food. It had been fun to watch the princess, but I hadn't gotten to see too much pain out of her, so I was looking forward to this. I was brimming anew with resentment after that dream reminded me of how they sold me out.

And so in a giddy mood, I cut the Dungeon Core to pieces.

System message: Title acquired: "Dungeon Master."

System message: "Monster's Blade of Hatching" unlocked.

"Oh? What's this? I think I unlocked a new soul blade. Let's see... Hmm... Oh, right, this is the first time I destroyed a Dungeon Core personally, I guess."

"Is that right, Master? Congratulations!"

"And to think I'd cleared out all those dungeons in the past. I can't believe I'm only getting this now."

The first time, I had been a bit of a goody two-shoes. In those days, if I came across a dungeon while out and about and defeated its boss, I would leave the Dungeon Core for the local lord or else report it to the Adventurers Guild. So this was my first time destroying a Dungeon Core myself, and immediately, I could tell that I'd gotten a lot of experience from it. I decided to leave my new title and soul blade for later and checked my experience while picking up the fragments of the core.

"Whoa... Twenty-five thousand experience—is this for real?"

What a steal. The Dungeon Core couldn't even move or fight back, and the experience I got from it was enough to pay off my debt and allow me to level up again. I considered this as I grabbed everything I needed off the dungeon floor and headed back outside, with Minnalis at my side.

"Mmm! It feels so good to be back in the sunlight again, Master!"

It took us five days to return to the surface from the Guardian Room. The destruction of the Core didn't mean that all the monsters had suddenly disappeared, so we had to deal with them on the way out, and it had taken longer than I expected.

"Too true. Humans have got to be out in the sun. It's not good for us to stay cooped up underground for weeks at a time."

"They say that long ago, the Spirits infused the sun's rays with the power of life. And it does seem that places that get more sunlight have better crops."

"That's probably because of photosynthesis... Wait, are there really places where the land is blessed by the Spirits? This is a fantasy world, I suppose..."

I'd really stretched myself thin the first time in order to get back to my world as quickly as possible. I'd never really stopped to think about how this world worked. Perhaps once my revenge was over, it would be nice to get into agriculture, start a little farm... It was difficult to think that far ahead, and I couldn't quite imagine myself in that position. I once had such clear dreams for the future back in school, before I came here. Now anything after the successful completion of my revenge was like a distant blur.

So yes. I suppose I was only going to live happily ever after once I took from my targets everything they had.

As I thought of the future and chatted with Minnalis, we ended up before the city walls. Sure enough, there were more monsters the closer we got to the city, and we could hear the howls of the garm and the strange cackling laughter of the goblins.

"Oh, whoopsie. Looks like we're a little late."

"Let us hurry, Master. We might be missing the best part!"

"You're right. Let's hustle."

I activated my Stealth skill so the monsters would ignore us and went to a vantage point with a clear view of the hole in the wall. We got as close as we could without being seen by the townspeople and perched ourselves on a big thick branch to gaze at the carnage below.

"Ooh, it's still going! Look at that! Wow, isn't this such a great spot?"

"It appears things have just started," noted Minnalis. "From what I can see, they've only captured a couple of people so far."

The hole, initially sized for just the two of us, was now large enough to have three carts side by side. I thought back to the last time, where it had been about the size of one cart, and chuckled to myself at how stupid the people living around there had been. Their idiocy had far exceeded my expectations.

By my reckoning, the herd of monsters attacking the city was about twice as large this time. Just as before, the Poison Garm had entered and was spreading its paralyzing poison before hunting the immobile townsfolk.

Now, some soldiers had heard the commotion and come over to fight it. The garm could only use its poison every once in a while, so for now, the two sides fought evenly. However, the monsters had their numbers and pressed the assault. One by one, the townspeople fell to the wolves' teeth and claws, or the goblins' wooden clubs, and were dragged away into the forest.

Once a solid group of adventurers were to turn up, they would drive the monsters away surely, but in the meantime, I wanted to see how things developed.

"Ha-ha, that Poison Garm isn't a bad leader. I wonder how many people they'll get before the adventurers show up. Want to make a bet?"

"You mustn't, Master. Alcohol, women, and gambling are the ruin of man. Let's just enjoy the view and have something to eat. Here you are."

"Ah, gracias."

Minnalis passed me some Ricoco berries that grew wild in the forests around here. They were a mysterious fruit that looked like blue apples but tasted like strawberries.

"Grassy...what?" Minnalis blushed.

"It means *thank you*. Oh, look, they got another one."

I bit into the sweet fruit as I watched the battle unfold. The soldiers weren't necessarily incompetent, but the hole had let so many monsters through that the town was being overrun.

"Gaaaargh! Nooo! Somebody! Gaaagh!"

It was hard to tell from a distance, but I recognized him as someone who sold me out to the princess last time.

"Help! Nooo! Somebody, help me! Help meeee!"

"Ha-ha-ha. I'm not falling for that one again. This time, I'm just gonna let the monsters eat you."

I watched as the man's feet were mauled by garm and his arms broken by goblin clubs. His screams were like music to my ears.

"Oh, Master. Isn't that woman one of them, too? I remember her from your vision."

"Hmm? Ahhh, that's his wife. Oh dear. Looks like she's surrounded by goblins. I believe we're about to see the goblins planting their seed. Poor thing."

"You're a terrible liar, Master. You always smile when you lie."

"Ah. Busted."

We cracked jokes as we watched the townsfolk suffering below. They weren't enough to earn my full attention, so it was fun to watch them being murdered for me.

"Hmm? Wait... Oh man, what are you doing?"

Suddenly, a man appeared on the scene. It was the weapon-shop owner I had met previously. His shop wasn't so close to the hole that it would be in danger. Why was he here?

"Hold on... No, get out of there, you idiot!"

He started swinging his sword pathetically at the monsters. It was hard to tell whether he was trying to save anyone or just messing around. When he got to one of the townspeople lying paralyzed on the ground, he gave them a small bottle. When they drank it, they got up to their feet and were able to run away. It must have been an anti-paralysis potion.

"What are you saving those scum for?! They're not worth it! You've got your shop to look after...!"

"Master, please stop. They'll see us!"

"Ugh...sorry."

At Minnalis's admonishment, I reined in my emotions and suppressed our presence once more. The weapon-shop owner continued to hand out potions and help the townspeople to safety.

Anti-paralysis potions were rather expensive. I had told him to stock up on them so he could be making a killing right now. He wasn't supposed to be handing them out for free.

"...Why can't you see? Those people aren't worth saving."

He'd given out over ten potions already. Even if the soldiers would reimburse him later, there's no way the townspeople were going to do the same. They were the type of people to say, *I didn't ask for your help.*

I knew the weapon-shop owner was in dire straits financially. This could cost him his store. But more than that, he was putting himself in danger. The only reason he could fight the monsters at all was because his dwarf blood gave him an edge stat-wise. The soldiers at least had training, but they were no adventurers, either.

So it was no surprise that just as he stopped to help a fallen girl, a goblin soldier snuck up behind him and was about to get the drop on him.

"Grrr, dammit!"

"Master!"

I jumped into action almost reflexively. Channeling mana into my legs, I used my newly upgraded Fleet-Foot and Air Step skills to dash directly toward them.

"Graaagh!"

"Wha—?"

I launched a full-speed kick at the goblin, not even a proper move, and blasted his head clean off, kicking up a cloud of dust as I landed.

"L-laddie! It's you!"

"Why are *you* here?" I spat at the befuddled weapon-shop owner. "There's no value in saving these spineless vermin. I know those potions aren't cheap—why are you throwing them away?"

He wasn't an idiot, and he knew what the people around here were like. He knew that using his potions on them meant giving them away for free.

"...Listen, bozo. I'm grateful an' all fer yer helpin' me an' that. But to say there's no value in savin' people is a step too far!"

"But look, they don't even thank you, and they run off without helping anyone else!"

"They're not all like that! An' I don't know what they're like till I save 'em, ain't it?"

"I know that! But they—"

Before I could say *betrayed me*, the weapon shop owner cut me off.

"Or are you sayin' it's fine if this lass gets eaten, is that it? You wanna see a little girl get killed?!"

Then for the first time, I looked down at the little girl who was trembling at my feet.

...So what if she got killed? These people betrayed me. They told me they were grateful to me, then turned right around and sold me out.

That's right, she betrayed me.

...She betrayed me? Did she really?

This little girl, quivering with fear on the ground... Did she really betray me?

"No...it's not her I care about..."

As I muttered my true feelings, there was a loud eruption of shouts that drowned out my words.

"*Tsk...* Looks like the cavalry's here."

Finally, a group of adventurers showed up. They were wearing mismatched armor that distinguished them from the uniformed soldiers.

"...Here, take this with my apologies and thanks. It should be more than enough to make up for all those potions you used," I said, tossing a single gold piece toward the weapon-shop owner. "But this is the last time I help you, understand? I've paid you back for everything you've done. Next time, you're on your own."

"Huh? Hey, lad!"

I didn't look back at the old man. I returned to Minnalis before anyone else showed up.

"Why did you go out there, Master?"

"It was that old man. He wasn't one of my enemies. I didn't want him to die here. That, and maybe I felt a little indebted to him from what happened the first time around."

"It's dangerous, Master. I know you're not a killer, but things are only going to get tougher from here on out. You can't let your emotions get the better of you."

Minnalis looked at me with cold eyes. It was clear she was prepared for the road to come.

"We're partners in crime, Master. I can't do it without you. Please promise me you won't put yourself in danger like that ever again."

"...I'm sorry, but I realized something. This...this isn't going to work."

Not everyone in this city had betrayed me. When the princess's men came knocking, asking for information on me, some feigned innocence and turned them away. A little girl shared her candy, even though she knew nothing about me. There were decent people in this land.

So this plan wouldn't work. I hadn't counted on getting those people involved.

"I can't let other people get caught in the cross fire of my revenge. This...this isn't right. There are too many innocent bystanders. They didn't do anything to deserve this. Why didn't I realize it sooner?"

I had crossed the line, and I was straying into madness. I had no qualms killing anyone if it was absolutely necessary to exact my revenge, but if I just started murdering civilians because it was easier, I was in real danger of losing the last sliver of my humanity. The last piece of myself that Leticia had given me. Without it, I was nothing more than a monster.

Revenge is an emotion, not an instinct. It's a part of our soul. Something a mindless beast could never understand.

I was going to kill the princess. Kill the king, the queen, the prime minister, the knight commander. I would show them no mercy. I was going to make them regret what they did and then keep going—show them just how cruel life could be before I snuffed them out entirely. There was no room for anything more. My revenge was to be flawless, immaculate, pristine.

So I had to be selective. I needed to choose who *really* needed to die, and I needed to think of a way to remove the chaff. No impurities. It had to be *refined*.

The weapon-shop owner. The little girl. They weren't my enemies, nor would killing them make my enemies suffer. They were impurities who had nothing to do with my revenge. But they didn't have to be collateral damage. This was an imperfect method. My focus had slipped.

I hadn't considered the costs and whether I was willing to accept them. I had simply acted on emotion and sown chaos.

Today's plan had been an absolute failure.

If I continued with the line drawn in the wrong place, I would never live to see my revenge completed.

"Let's go, Minnalis. We have a lot to think about if we want to come up with the perfect revenge. We're not murderers. We're not doing this for fun. We can't keep killing people if it doesn't advance our goals. Our revenge isn't some short-term plan; it's going to be a thing of beauty. There's so many other people who are more deserving of it."

With that, I turned my back on the city walls and began to walk away.

"You're off in your own little world, Master. I haven't finished talking yet."

"Aaau! Dat hurth, Linnaliff!"

Minnalis pinched my cheek as I tried to leave, shattering the cool end scene I was going for.

"I don't object to you rescuing the weapon-shop owner. I'm angry that you put yourself in danger to do it. Do you understand what I'm saying? You're still weak, Master. It was you who said we had to be discreet in the first place, remember?"

"I-I'm sowwy. Au'll be careful next time, I fwear..."

"...I really do care about you, Master. You know that, right? I can't bear this vengeance alone. You want to make our plan perfect? Then come up with an idea that doesn't require putting yourself in danger."

Minnalis sighed and released my cheek... I thought it was going to come off. I'm not kidding.

"So are we going to proceed as planned?" she asked.

"Yeah, we'll head north. We're going to Elmia, the academy town."

I looked back toward the city one last time. We would likely not be returning for a while.

The monsters that had not already fallen to the adventurers' blades were retreating into the forest. Once they no longer had the numbers, they didn't stand a chance. Soon enough, peace would return to the city.

"Just you wait. King, Queen, Princess, knights, and the rest of you scum. I'm gonna drag you all down to the depths of hell."

For whatever reason, I was given a second lease on life.

Last time, everyone walked all over me. Now it was my turn.

It was time to hit the road.

A road of revenge, with no destination—laughing at the mistakes I made before.

Even if only I knew this journey.

Even if I could never be proud of my new life.

At least I wouldn't be left to rot by the roadside like last time.

...I would laugh while walking the path of vengeance.

SIDE STORY

Minnalis's Plan:
Operation Engulfment

SHORT STORY

The Day of Tragedy

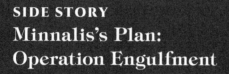

*W*ho is it you want to kill?"

That was the very first question my master had asked of me. Even as broken as I was, I realized that it was not what one would normally ask of a slave.

So I looked back into his eyes, and right then, I could tell he meant something. At the bottom of a dark pit of mud, there was a festering cloud and an unquenchable red-hot light.

Instinctively, I knew we were two of a kind.

"Who do you want revenge on?"

So when he asked that second question, I answered. Everyone who made me and my mother suffer.

"Isn't it obvious? Two is more fun than one. Two can come up with much better plans, put much more effort into torturing our targets, breaking them, grinding them down into mush. People who just want to kill are of no use to me, but you aren't like that, are you?"

Whether he meant to or not, he saved me by saying that. He gave me the strength and sustenance to keep my broken heart from falling apart completely. Like water on the seed of my revenge. When all I knew how to do was smolder in anger, he taught me new emotions and gave me new desires.

I wanted him. I wanted to be near him. I wanted to be useful to him.

I wanted to feel him, be with him, make him mine.

I think I fell in love with him.

Ah, I think I understand now how Lucia felt. Except my feelings are far stronger than hers, of course. That wicked little witch. I can use this love to nourish my vengeance. I was so lucky to fall in love, because now I know exactly how to grind her heart down into a sticky mess.

It would surely come in handy.

The demon living in my heart chuckled.

It had nearly been ten whole days since I first met Master. In the dungeon, I learned a new facet of what made him so great. He was far stronger than I was, even though he was only level 1. He showed me that true strength lay in more than simple stats.

Master told me that there were other, hidden stats, which the status screen didn't display, and that was where our differences lay.

I could feel myself becoming more like him in the way he conducted himself on the battlefield, in the way he swung his sword. But it wasn't enough. I needed to train harder.

"Nnnh…"

"Oh dear, I almost missed out on this rare opportunity."

After I had finished poisoning the Guardian Room as Master had asked, I pulled his sleeping body away from the wall and into my lap. I was thinking about my worries as I brushed his silky hair.

There was one other flame in my heart besides my revenge, and unfortunately, it seemed like it was going to take a long time to make him mine.

Fortunately, he seemed to take note of my feminine charms. I could feel his wandering gaze whenever I feigned MP drunkenness. On my lips, my breasts, my butt, my legs, my thighs, and the place in between them.

Of course, it wasn't as though he was ogling me all the time, but it didn't need to be that obvious for me to tell.
…Though it was hard to keep the act up when the only thing I wanted to do was smile.

In any case, it was too soon to tell him how I felt, because there was another who occupied my master's heart. The demon lord named Leticia.

She had been the one to save my master at his lowest point, just as he had saved me at mine.

Given all the things I learned when I had my vision of Master's life, I could guess he harbored feelings for her. But this time, after his do-over, their relationship no longer existed, and I didn't even need to ask to know that he didn't want her to be involved in our quest for revenge. In which case, he would soon be forced to draw a line between the Leticia he remembered and the one in this world. When that time came, I couldn't allow him to come to some strange conclusion like *No one else can ever replace her* and lock me out forever. That was why I couldn't be too forward with him right now.

"*After rejecting one woman, a man may go on to reject every other who comes his way, even after breaking up with the first woman.*" That's what I heard from a party of adventurers who came to my village one time.

Therefore, I had to wait until his relationship with the demon lord girl was well and truly in the past. Then I could get Master to start thinking of a new future and slip into a little me-sized hole in his heart. Until then, I had to be prudent and refrain from any outrageous behavior.

I had been using the MP drunkenness as a cover to gradually file away at his emotional defenses, whittling down his reluctance, nestling up close to his heart, waiting for that moment to arrive.

In the meantime, I needed to be a woman who was normally calm and collected and was embarrassed by the things she did while under the influence. That way, he wouldn't reject me out of hand.

"A new treasure—Master's hair!"

I carefully pulled the hair from my brush and placed it inside the round Squirrel's Blade of Holding. Master had allowed me to share in the power of this item, letting me amass a secret *collection* that even he couldn't access.

Right now, the finest item in my collection was this.

"Ahhh, there you are! Tee-hee! Mmm, so delicious."

I ran my tongue up the length of the wooden spoon Master had used.

Ahhh, I knew all that time and effort spent making this would pay off.

"Oh no, I mustn't. Perhaps I really did use too much MP after all."

I couldn't afford to let Master see me like this, with my lust obvious. Not only was it embarrassing, but even I could tell it was a little extreme, and I didn't want Master to be put off from me for good. The mere thought of it terrified me. I placed the spoon back and returned to watching Master's face as he slept.

"Mmmmh..."

The time went quickly, and at some point, he seemed to be having a nightmare. As much as I wanted him to feel the softness of my legs a little longer, it was about time to wrap up. Besides, I could still use the MP drunkenness as an excuse for having him in my lap.

I would hide the second flame inside me with a mask of shadow and work my way into the recesses of his heart like an encroaching poison. Then when the time was right, I would strike.

I would surround him with me, so there was nowhere for him to run. Once Leticia was out of his mind forever, he would be completely engulfed.

Until then, I would have to console myself with the small times like this when I could expand my collection.

Master, I won't let you escape from me, you know? Not before we exact our revenge, and not afterward, either. Not until my image is burned into those deep, dark eyes of yours.

Tee-hee! Hee-hee-hee-hee! ♪

The Day of Tragedy

Somewhere on the premises of the royal castle lay a building far away from any other that resembled a church of Lunaria. What was different about this building was that the normally blue-and-white color scheme, representing love and purity respectively, also included yellow, which represented the bravery of the royal family. Atop the front face of the building was the Y-shaped symbol that represented the Lunarian faith.

That building, built to hide information concerning the hero-summoning ritual, housed more robust security measures than anywhere else in the castle. It held soundproof barriers, antimagic barriers, physical barriers, all the highest level, such that it was incredibly complicated to access the inner sanctum.

In order to avoid having it be discovered from above, an illusion was cast on the air over the building so that to the untrained eye, it looked exactly like any other part of the castle grounds.

I, Princess Alicia Orollea, walked there as I clutched the necklace identifying me as the heir to the throne of the Orollea Kingdom.

"..."

The sound of boots on the marble floor echoed down the hallway, along with the noise of shuffling armor. I was accompanied by a unit of valiant knights whom the people looked up to. They were trained not for combat but in stylish sword techniques whose primary purpose was to dazzle the common folk. Most of them were sons of distinguished noblemen, and they trained only enough so that their skill with the sword did not drop and spent the rest of their time learning the ways of commanding a group of soldiers. In case of emergency, they would not be the ones on the front lines, and while they weren't quite as weak as the rank and file, they were near the bottom of the ladder when looking at the combat capabilities of the various knights available.

However, this was their time to shine. When the summoning ritual was complete, we would need to influence the hero onto our side, and that would be a lot easier without the likes of Commander Guidott scaring them off with his mere presence. First impressions were important. Make a good one, and the hero would be that much easier to control thereafter.

""Welcome back, Your Highness!""

The elite soldiers of Commander Guidott's battalion greeted us as we arrived. Only the royal family, the prime minister, and a few of the most elite knights were allowed to enter this secure facility. The national-security risk they presented was quite low, as the prime minister and the knights were all bound by a spell that prevented them from acting against the interests of the country or rebelling against the royal family. If they did, they would instantly die.

"At ease, knights," I told them. "Please lead the way."

""Yes, ma'am!""

The inside of the building was of simple make compared with the rest of the castle. Not shabby, but devoid of decorations such as paintings and suits of armor.

"You have prepared the requisite materials, I take it?"

"Yes, ma'am. As per your orders, the beastfolk slaves have been bought from the Grond Company in charge of Dartras and placed in the offering chamber."

"I see."

"However, we have gathered a small surplus, and there are currently thirty-four beastfolk over the room's capacity of two hundred."

"That won't be a problem. Two hundred is merely the ritual's minimum requirements. Any more will simply be used up without issue."

Besides, that, too, was part of the plan. These filthy beastfolk lives might not count for the same as those of humans, after all.

Then it happened.

"Hey, you! Get back here!"

"Hrh, hrh! Stay back!"

"*Tsk*, never a quiet moment…"

Suddenly, a young beastfolk boy came running toward me from farther down the hallway, pursued by several knights. The *Lupid* boy, as he appeared to be from his deep-black wolf ears, was dressed in nothing more than tattered rags, and around his wrists were the broken remains of his shackles. Blood covered his clothing and the small knife in his hand, and his face was visibly pale as he ran down the marble hallway, his chains ringing.

He seemed young, but still, he was one of those rotten beastfolk, and so his physical capabilities were high. Plus, he was armed. The knights appeared to be having trouble and likely did not resort to using magic for fear of damaging the building.

"Hrh?! Grrr!"

"Y-Your Highness?!"

The beastfolk boy saw me standing in his path and slowed to a halt. Trapped between me and the soldiers, he scanned his surroundings warily and growled, revealing his long, white fangs.

"What is the meaning of this?" I asked.

"Our apologies, Your Highness. This boy escaped from the tributary chamber," explained one knight with a nervous expression, embarrassed at his failure.

I wasn't fully aware of what was going on, but this was clearly a problem that needed to be dealt with.

"Child, my name is Alicia Orollea, princess of this kingdom."

"Your Majesty?! Please stay back; this boy is dangerous!"

"Please take a step back," I warned, gesturing for the knights to leave as I approached the boy.

"S-stay away from me!"

He growled like a dog and scowled at me as I ignored him and steadily drew nearer.

"Calm down. I'm not here to hurt you. I am your ally."

"Lies! You'll never trick me!"

"It's okay; trust me. I have the power to set you free."

The boy took a sudden step back, as if to run.

"If you flee now, my knights may end up hurting you. You must know that you cannot possibly escape from all of them."

"Grrr... No, that's not..." The boy's mind was suddenly mired in doubt.

"Come, have no fear. Put down that knife."

"Grrr...my friends... My friends are back there, too! Will you free them as well?"

"Of course. I'm sorry, it must have been so painful..."

I continued to get closer to the boy with a smile on my face, whereupon the knife fell from his hand and clattered onto the marble floor.

"I—I don't want to kill anybody... Waaah!"

The boy fell to his knees and cried. I crouched down and gently embraced him.

"Poor thing. Don't worry, it's all over now..."

I scooped the fallen knife off the ground before slitting the tendons of his unprotected feet.

"Graaaaaargh! Gah! Grrr!"

"...because you'll be dead soon enough."

I couldn't stand to touch the little runt any longer, so I pushed him away from me.

"He won't be running anywhere now. Hurry up and take him back to his room."

"Yes, ma'am!"

The knights jumped into action immediately at my words.

"Wh-why...?"

The boy could only manage a weak voice amid his tears.

"Why? Isn't it obvious? It's bad enough that you have the nerve to walk and talk like a human being, but for killing one of my knights, you're lucky I won't torture you to death."

"Grrr! Graaargh!"

I kicked his bleeding wounds to cause him as much pain as possible.

"Melt his flesh so the blood doesn't get everywhere. I don't want him to taint my halls more than he already has. Then get him back into the offering room."

"Yes, ma'am! Now hold still, you little runt! *Fireball*!"

"Gaaagggh! Aaaagh!"

The knight heeded my order and created as small a spell as he could muster to avoid collateral damage. After touching the ball of flame to the boy's leg and sealing the wound, the knight grabbed him by the hair and dragged him away.

"I can't believe I had to act in such a farce. I expect a full report later," I said to the other knights as I handed them the knife. "Be sure to bring appropriate compensation and commiserations to the deceased's family. He was killed bravely defending me from a vicious bandit."

"Your consideration is greatly appreciated, Your Highness. However, please refrain from acting in such a manner. It was extremely fortunate you were not harmed."

"Apologies. I shall take more care in future."

Admittedly, I had acted a little rashly.

"In any case, I seem to have dirtied myself with his blood. I simply cannot meet the hero in this state."

I looked down at my pure-white dress, which was now stained red with fresh blood.

"I'll have to change," I announced. "There should be a room somewhere around here."

"Yes, ma'am. I'll take you there at once."

I followed the female knight up the stairs and into the changing room.

"Ugh, I wish I could take a hot bath," I grumbled.

"Please accept my apologies, Your Highness."

"It's fine. Just thinking out loud."

I focused my thoughts elsewhere. It had taken no small amount of money and time to gather the tributes required for the ritual. There would be little chance of a do-over if this attempt were to fail.

After changing my clothes, the knight led me down into the summoning chamber. A magic circle was inscribed onto the floor within, and the environs were appropriately decorated to welcome the new hero. Rows and rows of knights were already lined up and waiting.

"Let us begin the summoning. I do hope we get a puppet that's easy to control."

I hated the fact that we had to call beings into this world and make a filthy mockery of the human form. However, I couldn't let my feelings impede the success of this ritual.

I am Princess Alicia Orollea, first in line to the throne of the Orollea Kingdom.

I sighed deeply, as if expelling the last traces of my emotion, leaving only pure, logical thought.

"It is sin enough simply to permit their existence in this world, so I hope they will be useful to us at the very least."

The Hero Laughs While Walking the Path of VENGEANCE a Second Time

VOLUME 2—COMING SOON!

"I know who I'll get my revenge on next."